I0600448

Red Scare

on Sunset

Charles Busch

A SAMUEL FRENCH ACTING EDITION

SAMUEL
FRENCH
FOUNDED 1830

SAMUELFRENCH.COM
SAMUELFRENCH-LONDON.CO.UK

FOR PRODUCTION ENQUIRIES

UNITED STATES AND CANADA
Info@SamuelFrench.com
1-866-598-8449

UNITED KINGDOM AND EUROPE
Plays@SamuelFrench-London.co.uk
020-7255-4302

Each title is subject to availability from Samuel French, depending upon country of performance. Please be aware that RED SCARE ON SUNSET may not be licensed by Samuel French in your territory. Professional and amateur producers should contact the nearest Samuel French office or licensing partner to verify availability.

MUSIC USE NOTE

MANNY KLADITIS   DREW DENNETT   SHAUN HUTTAR

PRESENT

The WPA Theatre
(KYLE RENICK, Artistic Director)
Production of

CHARLES BUSCH

IN

WITH

RALPH BUCKLEY   ROY COCKRUM
ANDY HALLIDAY   JULIE HALSTON   MARK HAMILTON
JUDITH HANSEN   ARNIE KOLODNER

SET DESIGN BY	COSTUME DESIGN BY	LIGHTING DESIGN BY
B.T. WHITEHILL	DEBRA TENNENBAUM	VIVIEN LEONE

SOUND DESIGN	WIG DESIGN	PRODUCTION STAGE MANAGER
AURAL FIXATION	ELIZABETH KATHERINE CARR	T.L. BOSTON

ASSOCIATE PRODUCERS	GENERAL MANAGEMENT	PRESS REPRESENTATIVE
MICHAEL COHEN	NIKO ASSOCIATES, INC.	SHIRLEY HERZ ASSOCIATES
BILL REPICCI		SAM RUDY
LYLE SAUNDERS		

WRITTEN BY
CHARLES BUSCH

DIRECTED BY
KENNETH ELLIOTT

CHARACTERS

RALPH BARNES

JERRY

PAT PILFORD

FRANK TAGGART

MARY DALE

MALCOLM

MARTA TOWERS

SALESGIRL

MITCHELL DRAKE

BERTRAM BARKER

R.G. BENSON

GRANNY LOU

OLD LADY

In the instances where a male actor plays a female role, the characterization must be totally realistic with not a suggestion of camp. If Granny Lou is played at all ridiculously for it's drag effect, an important, touching moment of the play will be lost.

SETTING

Hollywood, California

TIME

1951

PRODUCTION NOTE

Red Scare on Sunset was performed on a unit set consisting of several different levels and playing areas. Simple set pieces such as a chair, a settee or a desk with an overhanging lamp suggested various locales. There was also a large scrim that moved forwards and backwards that alternately suggested a large bay window for the beach house, a backdrop for the radio station, tilted on an angle it was a skylight for the Felson Studio. More detailed descriptions of the set pieces are described in the prop list.

Music and sound effects are very important in this play. Because the story takes place in so many diverse locales, the original production used quite sophisticated sound effects to give the feeling of the surf outside the beach house, the sounds of a pier in Santa Monica, the bells and clamor of a department store and the dreamlike sounds of Mary's nightmare. Popular music from the early fifties also helped establish the various moods of the play.

AUTHOR'S NOTE

Red Scare on Sunset was a fascinating experience for our company, Theatre-in-Limbo. It was our eighth play together and our first to delve into overtly political material. My field of expertise is storytelling and I'm certainly no political theoretician. Still, I've always been fascinated by the blacklisting period in Hollywood in the Fifties. It was a complicated time full of shifting loyalties, crises of conscience and tragic victims. To turn this into the stuff of comedy, I thought it would be mad fun to dramatize it from the point of view of the hysterical Right. The play takes the form of the red-baiting propaganda films that were made in the late Forties and early Fifties, films such as *Red Menace*, *I Married a Communist* and *My Son John*.

The play received an enormously emotional response. The audience was challenged to follow the fortunes of a heroine and her wacky best friend who believed in ideals that a contemporary audience feels contempt for. As a satirist, I like to shake up people's fixed attitudes. I was very surprised when some people took the play at face value and assumed, because I was playing the lead role of Mary Dale, that I shared her beliefs and was advocating blacklisting. Here I was performing in drag. How could I be championing the suppression of creative freedom? The irony of the play was clearly lost on them. Mary's smug, sanctimonious naming of names at the conclusion of the play was meant to be chilling. I thought it would be too obvious to have a blatantly villainous person do such an act. How much more scary to have nice, sweet Mary innocently destroy people's lives with her simple, Godfearing traditional American values. I'm sure there were many "nice ladies" who did such things without fully comprehending the effects of their actions. There are many "nice" people involved in similar conservative political activism today.

I think it's important not to simplify and sentimentalize history and reduce a complex period into a battle between good guys and bad guys. Extremism of both the Right and the Left deserves to be satirized. It was my hope in this play to create a mad comic world that sheds some insight into a grey, horrifying period in our country's history and to express my concern that those days are not so distant at all.

This play is dedicated with love to Meghan Robinson (1955-1990)

PROLOGUE

(Setting: The stage where The Pat Pilford Radio Show is broadcast. An "on the air" sign hangs above. The year is 1951. the place: Los Angeles.)

(At rise: **JERRY**, *a technician enters stage right with a cigarette in his mouth, carrying a mike stand and a script folded in his back pocket. He sets mike downstage center, exits stage right and returns with doorslam unit and sets it stage left. He adjusts mike.)*

*(***RALPH BARNES*** *enters.* **RALPH** *is an actor playing the folksy Uncle Sven on the radio show and is wearing a fake moustache and porkpie hat.)*

RALPH. *(looking over his script)* Hey there, Jerry.

JERRY. Afternoon, Mr. Barnes.

RALPH. Have you read this script?

JERRY. Nah, I never read 'em.

RALPH. Smart fella. You know they pay people to write this stuff?

DIRECTOR. *(voiceover)* Ralph, please. The studio audience.

RALPH. Just kidding, folks, Just kidding.

DIRECTOR. *(voiceover)* Has anyone seen Pat?

RALPH. Can't say that I've had the pleasure.

DIRECTOR. *(voiceover)* It's thirty seconds to air.

JERRY. I'll check her dressing room. *(exits right)*

RALPH. Would you like me to read her part?

(no response)

There goes my big chance.

JERRY. *(reentering stage right)* She's coming.

DIRECTOR. *(voiceover)* Fifteen seconds. Where is our star?

(PAT PILFORD enters stage right. She's an attractive blonde, the quintessential movie wisecracking, loyal sidekick, a clown who can't resist a double take or a pratfall. She's also a fierce right wing red baiter. PAT is both unlovable but impossible to dislike. She enters wearing an outrageous hat covered with fruit.)

PAT. I'm coming! I'm coming! I'm coming! You try running in this corset *(to the audience)* Believe it or not, I have a terrible weight problem. I always have to be on a diet. My old boyfriend, Herman, gave me a present. It didn't fit. And it was a Buick.

DIRECTOR. Five, four, three, two…

ANNOUNCER. *(voiceover)* The Veedol Motor Oil Program with Pat Pilford…

(applause/music)

…makers of Veedol Motor Oil, found wherever fine cars travel, present Miss Show Business, Pat Pilford. With Ralph Barnes, Emmaline Crane, Jimmy Stall and special guest stars Tony Martin, Dagmar, Slapsy Maxie Rosenbloom, Les Paul and Mary Ford. Yours truly Bill Simmons and Victor Arnold and his chiffon orchestra. *(music tag)* …And now your fabulous femme-cee, Pat Pilford.

PAT. Hello sweeties. Boy oh boy, do we have a show for you. I suppose I've always been stage struck. I'm the type of gal that when I open the refrigerator and the light goes on, I do twenty minutes. Now I simply must tell you…

(JERRY slams door.)

RALPH. *(using a comical Swedish accent)* Patty dear, may I speak to you for just a minute?

PAT. Oh Uncle Sven,

(applause)

I'm about to start my show. Is something the matter?

RALPH. I apologize. How would you like to go with me Saturday night to the Swedish folk dance marathon? What suspense? Can Olaf and Hildy dance the Glog and Shpickle for forty-eight hours?

PAT. I'm afraid I'll have to pass. Hold onto your chair. I've got a date Saturday night.

RALPH. Oh yumpin' yimminy. I'm as yolly as a yune bug dancing a yoyful yig. Is this a serious romance?

PAT. Sure is. His first glimpse of me was at the Beverly Hills Hotel when I was lying by the pool. I was being real seductive. He was desperate to meet me. I heard him whisper to his pal "get her."

RALPH. Now darlin', be careful. Sometimes I just worry about your choice in men.

PAT. Oh, you're thinking about Herman. He wasn't what you call "husband material." He was addicted to horse racing. When I took him to church, I had to keep telling him "It's Hallelujah, not Hialeah."

RALPH. I apologize for interfering, but I just have your best interests...

PAT. *(putting down her script)* I have to stop here.

RALPH. *(still acting)* I just have your best interests at heart...

PAT. I said stop. I cannot continue this show.

RALPH. *(retaining his accent)* Patty, dear, is there something I can do?

PAT. Yes, you can can the accent. You're not Uncle Sven. Fortunately you are no relation to me at all. You're Ralph Barnes, an actor, and as of now, an unemployed actor.

RALPH. *(dropping the accent)* I don't understand.

PAT. Then I shall make myself clear. You're fired. I will not perform another minute with anyone whose politics jeopardize...

RALPH. Pat, I'd be very careful choosing my next few words if I were you.

PAT. How are these words? I'm giving you the pink slip, bub.

RALPH. I can't believe this is happening. Pat, we are on the air.

PAT. I don't care if we're in the air, I will not continue until you leave this studio. I'm waiting.

RALPH. *(mortified)* I will. I will leave. I can't believe this. This is unbelievable. *(He exits right bewildered.)*

PAT. My dear audience. I apologize for what must seem to you cruel and unprofessional behavior. A long time ago, I devoted my life to bringing you, the American public, wholesome, clean entertainment for the entire family and I will be darned if I'll let some cynical, agitating New York actor come between me and that pledge. Now I say this to you, not as Pat Pilford, funny lady but as a concerned citizen and long-time friend, the time has come for all of us to clean house.

(blackout)

ACT I

Scene 1

(The beach house of movie stars **MARY DALE** *and* **FRANK TAGGART**. *There is a chair stage right and a small settee stage left with a coffee table in between. On either side of the stage are platforms that can be used as table surfaces. Late afternoon, tea time.* **PAT PILFORD** *is seated with* **FRANK**, *a handsome and intense man in his mid-thirties.)*

FRANK. I'm surprised to see you. That was some havoc you created on your show this afternoon. The whole town must be talking about it.

PAT. You should have seen the press buzzing around. It was like they had Mexican jumping beans in their jockstraps. All I did was fire an actor.

FRANK. On the air and nearly denouncing him as a communist.

PAT. I'm sorry. I just hate phoniness. Anyway, Frank, what's done is done, no looking back, tomorrow's another day.

FRANK. But this is serious. You've destroyed a man's career.

PAT. He can always get a job with the Moscow Art Theatre. Look, I don't want to talk about it. *C'est la vie.* Frank, I am very impressed with this house. I'm so glad Mary wouldn't let me see it till it was finished

FRANK. Well, it's not my taste but you know Mary. She's always wanted a real movie star beach house in Santa Monica. Can I fix you a drink? Pat, you're a Rob Roy girl if I recall.

PAT. A shot of hootch would be tempting but I better say nix. I'm Mary's guest for tea and that girl's a walking breath test.

FRANK. If it's all right with you, I'll fix myself one.

(He goes to a small liquor tray stage right and makes himself a drink.)

PAT. Starting rather early these days, aren't you Frank?

FRANK. These are tough days.

PAT. They sure are, boy, they sure are. Hollywood ain't the boom town it once was. Not the way it was when I landed here in '35. It's the big T, television. Every actor in town is looking at his bank book and sweating. I applaud your confidence in building this dream house. I don't want to be rude but I've seen the numbers on your last few pictures. My little nephew has crayon drawings that have been more widely seen.

FRANK. I appreciate that, Pat. I could have told the studio those films would flop. The public is sick of that same romantic crap the studios have feeding them for years.

PAT. That's right. You're from the old Give-the-folks-a-message-and-ram-it-down-their-throats school of entertainment. Well, not me, brother, I like to leave 'em laughing. This is my message and here's how I send it. *(She makes a wild comic face.)*

FRANK. I imagine you weren't laughing when you lost the SAG election last month.

PAT. No Frank, I wasn't. In fact, I wept and not for me, Frank. I wept for the union. I bet I didn't have your vote.

FRANK. I'm sorry. I just didn't think you were experienced enough to be President of the Screen Actors Guild.

PAT. Experience! I have been in this business since I was four years old. Vaudeville, the Follies, radio, forty-two films and believe you me, I know why I lost that election. It's the red influence of Mr. Stalin and Mr. Lenin that has infiltrated every corner of our industry!

FRANK. Pat, I really don't want to discuss politics with you. It upsets Mary and she should be down any minute.

PAT. You don't seem to mind discussing politics with others.

FRANK. What's that supposed to mean?

PAT. Oh nothin'. It's just that you have a reputation for having passionate political beliefs. Weren't you quite active in liberal causes in your New York theatre days?

FRANK. We all were. It was the spirit of the times. We suffered so during the depression.

PAT. You're going back to New York soon, aren't you?

FRANK. You *are* well informed. Perhaps I *should* have voted for you. Yes, I'm going back to do a play.

PAT. Will Mary be joining you?

FRANK. I doubt it. She's got a string of pictures lined up.

PAT. It's the old "Star is Born" scenario. One goes up and the other goes down.

FRANK. *(matter of factly)* Pat, fuck you.

> *(***MARY DALE*** *enters stage left Door.* **MARY** *is a gracious woman, a star who is also the perfect wife. She is wearing a magnificent green chiffon dress covered with pink roses. She is Scarlett O'Hara at the barbecue circa 1951.)*

MARY. Pat, precious. *(She crosses to her and kisses her.)* Frank, darling. *(She starts cross to him. notices him drinking, makes a horrified face but then tries to put on a bright expression. She crosses to him and kisses him.)* Forgive me for being late. When one has tea with the girls, one dresses to the nines.

PAT. Well, honey, you're dressed to the ninety nines. There is no one in Hollywood with more tone.

MARY. *(with a gentle mocking tone)* You're sweet, but Pat, that hat…

PAT. Leave my hat alone. I'm a low comic. I'd be more at home in baggy pants.

MARY. I heard you fired Ralph Barnes.

PAT. Well you heard right.

MARY. *(with true sincerity)* Poor darling, I know how hard it is for you to fire people.

PAT. *(very grateful)* Thank you Mary, I appreciate that. It's always hard and I shed tears. Now please, let's not say another word about it. Frank was telling me about the play he's doing in New York.

MARY. *(suddenly sad)* He could be gone for months. Don't know how I'll bear it.

FRANK. You'll be busy filming.

MARY. *(suddenly happy)* Yes, a biography of Lady Godiva. I've always felt such an affinity for Eleventh Century England. It's a marvelous script. Really illuminates those troubled times. And we have terrific musical numbers. I wanted the studio to cast Frank as the Lord of Coventry but…he didn't think the role was right for him.

FRANK. You mean the studio didn't think we had the right chemistry on screen.

MARY. What am I to do with my brooding young man?

FRANK. I just hate this town and everything it stands for.

PAT. Be careful, Mary. He may go to New York, and not come back.

MARY. I'll get him back. When I told that preacher "till death do us part," believe me I never spoke dialogue with more conviction. *(takes **FRANK**'s arm)* Pat, I found myself a man, do you hear, a *man* and I'm not going to let this one get away, ever.

FRANK. *(draining his drink)* Well, you're gonna have to let me go for a little while. I'm due at the photo gallery in forty five minutes. I'll be glad when I'm an old character man and don't have to take these phony glamour photos. Give a kiss, baby.

(They kiss.)

MARY. Oh darling, remember we're having dinner with the Gradys this evening. Cocktails at seven.

FRANK. Oh boy. I can't, Mary.

MARY. Why not? We've had this planned for weeks. They're counting on us.

FRANK. You'll have to go without me. I'm meeting with my agent to discuss a new image for me. He says it's urgent.

MARY. But surely you could have told me this earlier.

FRANK. It came up very suddenly.

PAT. Sort of from left field, so t' speak.

FRANK. *(glares at* PAT*)* Look, I've gotta run. I'm sorry, Mary. I am. *(He exits stage right door.)*

MARY. I worry about him, Pat. I worry about him.

*(*MALCOLM*, the houseboy, enters stage left door.* MALCOLM *is a good looking fella in his late twenties, though high-strung and pale.)*

MALCOLM. Mrs. Taggart, should I serve tea now or would you prefer waiting till your other guest arrives?

MARY. *(to* PAT*)* Are you famished or shall we wait?

PAT. Oh, it don't matter. A cup of tea is a cup of tea. How're things going, Malcolm?

MALCOLM. Quite well, Miss Pilford. You're looking in full bloom.

PAT. Can't complain.

MARY. Weren't you both working at Republic at the same time?

PAT. Oh yes. Malcolm was in the make-up department when I did a picture there.

MALCOLM. *(matter of factly)* Indeed. Miss Pitford is the reason why I'm not working at Republic anymore.

MARY. Pat, did you have Malcolm fired?

PAT. Let's just say that I didn't care for the shade of red he was pushing.

MARY. That dark lipstick you wear is dated. But Malcolm, I'm glad you're free to work for me. I don't know what I'd do without you.

MALCOLM. That's very kind of you, Mrs. Taggart.

MARY. Miss Pilford knows our little secret that Frank has something of a drinking problem. You don't know how grateful I am to Malcolm. How many nights he's had to strip Frank naked and hold him under the shower. I owe Malcolm a lot.

MALCOLM. Think nothing of it, Mrs. Taggart. It was my pleasure. Will that be all for now?

MARY. For the moment.

MALCOLM. Excuse me. *(He exits stage right door.)*

PAT. *(sighs)* I suppose some women have a passion for pansies.

MARY. What are you talking about?

PAT. Surely you know that Malcolm is that way. *(She licks her pinky and wipes her brow.)*

MARY. Because he isn't married. Really Pat, haven't you ever heard of a bachelor? My Uncle Maurice lived with his best friend Cyril for thirty-two years. They had the most beautiful home in Indianapolis. You've never seen such gardens and they were definitely not that way. *(She licks her pinky and wipes her brow.)*

PAT. *(irritated)* Mary Dale, you are just too good to be true.

MARY. Besides it's none of our business what people do in the privacy of their own homes.

PAT. Mary, you are so wrong. We must know who's boffing who.

MARY. Pat, such language.

PAT. *(getting all riled up)* It's time to grow up and smell the lavender. That kind of behavior undermines the core of our entire system, the sanctity of the American family. Girl, there's strange sex going on in homes throughout this fair city and it's my duty as a citizen to expose it. People are sodomizing each other at the drop of a hat. The government must have this information. We must drag them out into the light!

MARY. Next you'll be wanting FBI cameras in our bedrooms.

PAT. Why not? I've nothing to be ashamed of. Roll film! Cut! Print it!

MARY. *(sincerely)* Pat, I do envy your grasp of the issues challenging our world.

PAT. *(takes her hand)* You are just a darling little kitten with a heart as big as the Hollywood Bowl. I'll do the big thinking for both of us. So Lambikins, who's our mystery guest for tea?

MARY. Marta Towers.

PAT. Marta Towers! Are you crazy?

MARY. Why? Do you know her?

PAT. Marta Towers is the most notorious pinko in Hollywood.

MARY. Oh, she has a few liberal friends.

PAT. Marta Towers has had more Russians in her than the Kremlin.

MARY. *(covering her ears)* Pat, please.

PAT. Well, I won't speak to her. Imagine inviting me here along with that woman. She holds everything that Pat Pilford stands for with contempt.

MARY. She's a fine actress and a lovely girl. I've only met her a handful of times and for a housewarming gift, she sent us a complete set of silver bar equipment.

PAT. An ice bucket, a shaker and a hammer and sickle.

MARY. Stop that.

(doorbell rings)

And none of that pink talk when she's here. That's just nasty gossip, you'll see.

(MALCOLM enters stage right door.)

MALCOLM. Mrs. Taggart, Miss Towers has arrived.

(MALCOLM exits stage left door and MARTA TOWERS enters stage right door. MARTA is a pretty woman, demure and ladylike but with an inner fire.)

MARY. Marta dear.

MARTA. Mary, your house is exquisite. Makes my little place look like a shack.

MARY. I can't believe that. Let me guess your style. French provincial?

MARTA. I have no style. It's just a mish mash of furniture I've picked up around the world on my travels. I do have one prize possession. A genuine nineteenth century Russian samovar.

MARY. I'm pink with envy. I mean green with envy. Oh, I'm so rude. Do you know Pat Pilford?

MARTA. Who doesn't? You're an institution like Southern California Gas.

*(**MALCOLM** enters stage left door with a tray of tea and crumpets.)*

MALCOLM. Tea, ladies.

MARY. Over here, dear. There's nothing like a spot of tea on a cold Los Angeles afternoon.

PAT. Aren't we terribly grand. I knew this dame when she was Dale Evans' stand-in.

MARY. I never was.

MALCOLM. *(offering crumpets to **MARTA**)* Would you like one, Miss Towers?

MARTA. They do look delicious, but alas I just started a diet

MARY. *(pouring tea for **MARTA**)* You, you're thin as a rail.

MARTA. Well, perhaps I will have a nosh.

MARY. A nosh?

MARTA. That's a Yiddish expression. A bite to eat.

PAT. What kind of roll is this?

MARY. An English crumpet. *(to **MARTA**)* Cream and sugar, dear?

MARTA. No, thank you.

MARY. *(handing **MARTA** her cup)* You know, I'm currently filming a biography of Lady Godiva and when I take on a role I immerse myself completely in that world.

At this moment, I am utterly convinced that I'm living in the Eleventh Century.

MARTA. I suppose all actors are a little *meshugana*.

(**MARY** *pauses for a beat, not quite comprehending* **MARTA** *but then shrugs it off.*)

PAT. Marta, were you born in this country?

MARTA. Indiana born and raised.

MARY. *(relieved)* Really. I'm a fellow hoosier. I should have known. There's nothing foreign about you. You're as fresh and wholesome as an Indiana corn field. *(hands* **PAT** *her tea, pours her own cup and lifts it to sip)*

MARTA. It's been a problem. I long to play an exotic vamp but each time I do, I fall flat on my *tuchus*.

(**MARY** *nearly chokes on her tea.*)

MARTA. My, these are scrumptious.

MARY. Are you much of a cook?

MARTA. Yes, I adore cooking. As a matter of fact, I've been volunteering my services at a soup kitchen downtown.

MARY. Really?

MARTA. It's a terrible sight to see these once proud men reduced to poverty by a system that's failed them.

PAT. *(holds two crumpets over her breasts)* Hey, Mary, who's this? Gypsy Sara Lee.

MARY. *(laughs)* Oh Pat...

PAT. *(puts crumpet halves over her eyes)* Little Orphan Annie.

MARY. *(laughing)* Pat, stop. You're incorrigible. Marta, you were saying...

MARTA. Yes. Only last week at the soup kitchen, I met a man, a former GI who risked his life for this country and yet found himself a pariah, unable to get a bank loan, unable to find a job. He told me his wife...

PAT. Hey, Mary. *(She puts the crumpet in the center of her forehead like a doctor's light.)* Calling Dr. Kildare.

MARY. *(hysterical with laughter)* Pat, please. Marta, the GI told you what?

MARTA. Well he...he said his wife left him because–

(**PAT** *holds two crumpets over her ears.*)

PAT. Clark Gable.

MARTA. He said she...

PAT. *(stands up and holds the two crumpets on her crotch like testicles)* Hey Stella!

MARY. *(bent over with laughter)* Pat, please... *(wiping tears of laughter from her eyes)* Marta, you've really given me food for thought. Terribly disturbing. Girls! I just got back my snapshots from Bermuda. You must see Frank posing with all the little natives. It's darling. (**MARY** *exits to the bedroom.*)

PAT. *(sipping her tea)* I hear in Russia they drink their tea out of a glass.

MARTA. Yes.

PAT. Ever been there, Marta?

MARTA. A few years ago I did visit the Soviet Union. It was a fascinating experience.

PAT. *(with false sincerity)* I bet. Inspirational.

MARTA. In its way.

PAT. Sort of inspired you to want to see their way of life over here?

MARTA. We could learn some things from the Soviets.

PAT. Such as denying the freedom of speech?

MARTA. I wonder if we really have that freedom.

PAT. You bet your Continental Congress we do. Every crackpot in the land has his say. That's the problem. Why must everyone have a voice?

MARTA. Are you advocating censorship?

PAT. Yes! Ideas *must* be censored. Why can't people *understand* that concept?

(**MARY** *enters looking very perplexed holding a passport.*)

PAT. Mary, what's wrong?

MARY. I was looking for the snapshots in Frank's sock drawer and I found this passport.

MARTA. Is it Frank's?

MARY. I don't know. It's an old passport, outdated and it's Frank's photo.

PAT. So?

MARY. Only the name isn't Frank Taggart born in Minnesota. It says this person was born in the Ukraine and his name is…Moishe Nisowitz.

(blackout)

Scene 2

(That evening. The pier at Playa del Rey. **FRANK** *is seen waiting for someone on the lonely pier. He lights a cigarette. A woman appears in a trench coat and approaches him. It's* **MARTA TOWERS**.*)*

FRANK. I was afraid you wouldn't come. I had a helluva time getting out of the house. Mary thinks I'm with my agent. Marta, you looked very mysterious coming out of the fog. Mysterious and beautiful.

MARTA. Not by Hollywood standards. I've been told that the camera brings out odd things in my face.

FRANK. What does a cold metal thing like a camera know about a beautiful woman.

MARTA. Frank, we're not shooting a scene. You don't have to seduce me. I came to this dreary pier in God forsaken Playa del Rey because I wanted to. Now I want you to kiss me.

FRANK. Request granted.

(They kiss.)

MARTA. Have you thought about my proposition?

FRANK. Yeah, I have. I can't get it out of my mind.

MARTA. And?

FRANK. I…I don't know. It's what I'm starving for.

MARTA. Take the leap, Frank. We both know it's what you crave.

FRANK. It's my every fantasy but do I have it in me? Can I really go that far?

MARTA. Frank, dive in, get wet, get yourself dirty and do as I say, take a method acting class.

FRANK. You've got to understand, Marta. I was trained in light Broadway comedies. It was drummed into my head over and over, sincerity and timing equals talent.

MARTA. A cheap bourgeois simplification. There is no art without the soul, without the gut. Study Tolstoy and Turgenev and they will tell you the same.

FRANK. I've never been with a woman like you before.

MARTA. You mean with half a brain.

FRANK. You mustn't talk about Mary that way.

MARTA. Loyalty is admirable when it's directed at the right people and the right ideas. Misguided when it's wasted on idiots and tired clichés.

FRANK. Mary is a wonderful girl, the perfect wife.

MARTA. I'm sure she is but you've outgrown her. I'll admit she's not malicious but in her innocent way, she's dangerous. She's holding you back from becoming the artist we know you can be.

FRANK. Can an actor really be an artist?

MARTA. Oh yes, Frank. But you can't be content with superficialities. You must dig and search within yourself. I see in you such possibilities. I hope you won't think I'm being too pushy but I see us as a great acting team.

FRANK. You do?

MARTA. Oh yes, Frank. I see us returning to the theatre, away from all this silliness and act great roles in great plays. Think of how much fun we'd have doing *The Lower Depths, The Weavers, Saint Joan of the Stockyards.*

FRANK. *(getting excited) The Weavers,* yes.

(She tries to kiss him. He breaks away.)

No, I can't do this. I can't betray Mary.

MARTA. *(wrapping her arms around him) The Wild Duck, Baal, When We Dead Awaken, Blood Wedding, The Ghost Sonata, No Exit.*

FRANK. I'll do it. Where do I go?

MARTA. The Yetta Felson Studio. Sunset at La Brea. Tomorrow at eight. Frank, trust me, you'll never be the same.

(blackout)

Scene 3

(Late that night. MARY and FRANK's home. FRANK stumbles in drunk. He sits down and struggles to take off his shoe and can't. MALCOLM enters in his bathrobe.)

MALCOLM. Mr. Taggart, I thought I heard you come in.

FRANK. *(focused on his shoe)* I can't...this thing's...I...

MALCOLM. Here let me.

(MALCOLM kneels down and unties FRANK's shoes and takes them off.)

FRANK. Sorry I woke you up.

MALCOLM. That's all right. I was just worried that you'd hurt yourself. Here, let me massage your foot. You like when I do that.

FRANK. *(relaxing)* Oh yeah...like that. Were you in bed?

MALCOLM. It's after two in the morning. It's not unusual for a person to be in bed. Actually I was reading. I won't tell you what I was reading. I wouldn't want to shock you.

FRANK. Didn't we give you that robe?

MALCOLM. Yes you did. Last Christmas. From you and the missus. You're a very generous man. It's pure silk, see? *(He lifts up part of the robe exposing his bare thigh.)* It feels really good cause you know, I'm nude under here.

FRANK. *(not really listening)* Is that so?

MALCOLM. Yes I am. *(gets up and massages FRANK's shoulders)* I always sleep in the raw. It's handy since I never know when I'll have to throw you in the shower.

FRANK. Malcolm, you're all pal, a real guy.

MALCOLM. I'm also part woman.

FRANK. *(sobers up for a moment)* Whaaa?

MALCOLM. *(shifting gears)* I said "You've been with a woman." I can tell.

FRANK. Shhhh. And what a woman. Brains, brains, brains.

MALCOLM. I've got an idea. I'm going to take you to my room so we don't disturb the missus and I'm gonna give you a complete alcohol rub down. It's gonna feel so good.

FRANK. No, too messy.

MALCOLM. Don't worry. I'll take off my robe so it won't get ruined. We're just two guys. You won't mind if I'm also nude.

FRANK. No rub down.

MALCOLM. Don't give Malcolm a hard time. Bad boys get spanked. These pants are coming off, now. *(He begins unfastening* FRANK*'s pants.)*

*(*MARY *enters in pajamas and marabou trimmed mules. "Hers" is inscribed on her pajama top pocket.)*

MARY. Frank?

MALCOLM. *(standing up)* Mrs. Taggart. he's done it again.

MARY. *(with true sympathy)* And awakened you from a sound sleep. I'm so sorry, Malcolm.

MALCOLM. That's all right, Mrs. Taggart. Better me than you.

FRANK. Malcolm, my friend, fix me a scotch.

MARY. *(to* MALCOLM*)* No, you don't. Frank, you're drunk.

FRANK. Don't be upset, Mary.

MARY. Malcolm, you can go back to bed.

MALCOLM. Are you sure you don't need me? It can be hard getting those clothes off him.

MARY. I can undress him myself. Goodnight Malcolm and thank you.

MALCOLM. Well...goodnight then.

(He starts to exit. MARY *turns her back to him and* MALCOLM *makes an ugly face frustrated that she interrupted his possible seduction of* FRANK. *He exits.)*

MARY. Really Frank, how many times must you wake up the servants and force them to handle you in this drunken state.

FRANK. Layoff, will ya. I only had a few beers. I'm not that tight. Don't make me feel like I'm being watched by the FBI. Go back to bed, Mary.

MARY. Well, since you're as sober as a judge, perhaps it's a good time to show you this. *(She takes out the passport.)*

FRANK. What is it?

MARY. A passport belonging to one Moishe Nisowitz.

FRANK. **(FRANK** *explodes and shakes her furiously by the shoulders.)* Where did you find that? Give that back to me! *(about to strike her, then catches himself in horror)* Good God.

MARY. You wanted to strike me.

FRANK. I wouldn't have. I couldn't.

MARY. Frank, I'll believe anything you tell me. But please give me some explanation of what this means and why my discovery of it would cause you to nearly harm me. *(She hands him the passport.)*

FRANK. What can I say? This passport does belong to me. I am Moishe Nisowitz and it's true I was born in the Soviet Union.

MARY. Then everything you told me is a lie.

FRANK. I was afraid if you knew the truth you wouldn't marry me. My parents escaped to this country when I was two years old. We settled on the lower east side of New York. I loved this country and I always felt I belonged more to it than to my parents. So when they both died, I gave myself a new American name and a new past.

MARY. *(rushing into his arms)* Darling, I love you so. Despite everything. But please, let's not have any more secrets. You do love me, don't you? That isn't a lie, is it?

FRANK. Of course not. I love you so very much.

MARY. Because you know, if I ever found out you didn't love me, I think I'd kill myself.

FRANK. Mary, don't say such a thing.

MARY. I would, I would kill myself. When I love, I love completely. It's my life. It's who I am. Hold me darling. Hold me tighter. I like it like this. How did your meeting go with your agent?

FRANK. Not bad. He wants to lean me more towards comedy. But it's a tough sell. The studio doesn't think I'm funny. I hate comedy. How was your tea party with Pat and Marta? Did they come to blows?

MARY. They seemed to hit it off fine. But I don't know, there's something about Marta that bothers me. I don't know what it is. I'm tired. Let's get to bed.

FRANK. What's wrong with Marta? She's certainly been a friend to you.

MARY. She gave us lovely bar equipment although considering your proclivities; I would have preferred a blender for milk shakes. No, I wouldn't call her a great pal. Coming to bed?

FRANK. Shortly. I just don't see where you come off criticizing a woman who's done nothing more than want to befriend you.

MARY. I simply said there was something about her that bothers me.

FRANK. It's just that in this town everyone passes quick judgments on people. This guy isn't funny, this woman should be shunned.

MARY. I didn't say Marta should be shunned. But truth to be told, I find her humorless. And that certainly shows in her comedy playing.

FRANK. I know she can't compete with the glittering wit of a Pat Pilford.

MARY. Pat Pilford is a comedy legend and my best friend. I had no idea you were so devoted to Marta Towers.

FRANK. *(with mounting anger)* I don't like your tone, Mary. But it's my opinion that Marta Towers is one of the finest dramatic actresses gracing this artistic wasteland we call motion pictures.

MARY. The studio only signed *La Divine* because she was sleeping with the head of publicity.

FRANK. *(shouting)* Did Pat tell you smutty gossip?

MARY. Frank, listen to us, we're nearly arguing. Now, please, let's end this conversation and go to bed. After all, tomorrow is a rather important day.

FRANK. Tomorrow?

MARY. January seventeenth. The anniversary of the day we first kissed.

FRANK. Oh yes.

MARY. Now I hope you haven't forgotten we have reservations at Ciro's tomorrow night.

FRANK. Mary, I…

MARY. Frank, you haven't…

FRANK. I know it's awful but Marta said tomorrow night she could get me into her method acting class at the Yetta Felson Studio. They're very fussy about who they let in to observe. It's a great opportunity for me, Mary.

MARY. *(quietly)* I see. Of course, I am disappointed but I know how much this means to you.

FRANK. You're a great girl, Mary.

MARY. Couldn't I come with you? Surely they'd let me observe too.

FRANK. I don't think so.

MARY. But why not? I could hardly be called an amateur. I've made twelve pictures in three years.

FRANK. That's not the point, Mary.

MARY. What is the point, Frank? I'm not good enough. Do they look down their noses at your little wife who last year had two films on Variety's list of top moneymakers. Should I be ashamed of that?

FRANK. Mary, don't get worked up. It's just that they do a different kind of acting.

MARY. My kind of acting comes from the heart. My high school dramatics coach, Miss Helen Phipps, said I acted with the simple pure belief of a child. I'll compete any day with those pretentious intellectuals with their grunting and sweating.

FRANK. Mary, you sound foolish. Great acting is uncovering depths of emotion that dare to be ugly, even repulsive. It's the exposure of the self in all of its raw truth.

MARY. Can I help it if I'm pretty and have a flair for fashion. I'm terribly serious about my acting. I know everything about Lady Godiva, what she thinks, feels, wears. I swear if I was konked over the head this minute, her life would pass before my eyes.

FRANK. Mary, just face it. You're a movie star, not an actress. You wouldn't know Chekhov from Chill Wills.

MARY. Well, that does it! That does it! *(She runs into the bedroom.)*

FRANK. Mary, forgive me. It was a terrible thing to say.

MARY. *(enters carrying his pillow and blanket)* Tonight Frank Taggart or Moishe Nisowitz, whoever you may be, you sleep on the sofa. As of this moment, our twin beds are off limits.

FRANK. You don't have to worry. *(He grabs his coat.)* And another thing, if you've read your history books, your precious Godiva was nothing but a two bit whore. I'll amend that. All women are whores.

MARY. Buster, Godiva was a lady and so am I. Now get out!

FRANK. With pleasure.

(FRANK exits leaving MARY alone. forlorn and confused.)

(blackout)

Scene 4

(Bullocks Department Store, the next day. **PAT** *is revealed down right when lights come up.* **MARY** *is in the changing room.* **SALES GIRL** *enters stage left door. She crosses to* **PAT**.*)*

SALES GIRL. Miss Pilford, is anyone waiting on you?

PAT. Yes thank you. My friend is in the try on room.

SALES GIRL. You really ought to take a gander at some of our new cashmere sweaters. They are simply to die for. There's one with a collar covered in gold paillettes that screams out your name.

PAT. Oh honey, tell it to pipe down. My friend is trying to make me more "refeened."

SALES GIRL. Pardon me for saying this, but I listen to you on the radio every week and you are the only one with the courage to speak out on the red issue. Those commies ought to be wiped off the face of the earth. *(giggles)* Now if you'll excuse me Miss Pilford, I can see brassieres pointing at me. *(She exits stage right door.)*

*(***MITCHELL DRAKE*** *enters stage left door. He is an attractive, dark-haired man in his late thirties, an odd mixture of the intellectual, the macho and the dangerous.)*

MITCHELL. Ah, then it is you, Pat

PAT. Mitchell Drake.

MITCHELL. *(charming)* I saw the legs. Still better than any race horse and then I recognized the voice. Once heard, never forgotten.

PAT. What are you doing here in the ladies department at Bullocks? Oh, the perfume counter. A special gift for a special lady.

MITCHELL. You've got all the answers, don't you Pat?

PAT. I've got a helluva lot on you.

MITCHELL. I could say the same.

PAT. What brings you here to the Pueblo?

MITCHELL. There seems to be a demand for my services here in Hollywood. Perhaps the boys upstairs are starting to realize great screenwriters don't grow on orange trees.

PAT. I thought the great playwright would never leave New York.

MITCHELL. The great playwright needed a change of scenery.

PAT. Well, what sort of purchase do you have in mind? A large bottle of French perfume or a small vial of toilet water?

MITCHELL. Oh, something small. The lady is just a passing fancy. And she's passing quicker every second.

PAT. Oh, so you think we're ready for a second act, Mitch?

MITCHELL. I think we've had a long enough intermission, yes.

PAT. I nearly didn't survive the first act curtain.

MITCHELL. It wasn't all drama. We had fun. Those were exciting days for us in New York. Me writing sketches for the Follies and you wringing every laugh out of them. You were great. Great at everything. I'm going to be in town for a while. Shall we take advantage of the situation?

PAT. Taking advantage are good words to describe an affair with you. No, Mitchell, edit me out of any of your second act ideas.

MITCHELL. Oh, that's right. You're a great believer in censorship. You'll come around, Pat. Why fight it? You know you'll enjoy it. You always do.

(**SALES GIRL** *enters stage right door holding a foolish hat with pompoms jutting into the air.*)

SALES GIRL. Sir, is there anything I can help you with?

MITCHELL. No, I don't think so. I'll wait on that gift. Goodbye, Pat.

(He exits stage left door.)

SALES GIRL. Miss Pilford, I thought this little chapeau might intrigue you.

PAT. Oh, I don't know, dear. It's a bit too "Minnie Mouse on a bender."

(MARY enters stage right through curtains carrying garments and boxes.)

MARY. This is terrible, Pat. Here we are giving you a fashion makeover, and I go on a spending spree. *(She notices the hat in the salegirl's hand.)* Ah, that hat. It's so delectable. How much? Don't even tell me. Pat, this is your day.

PAT. We should just forget it I'm never going to be chic. It's like putting a Dior on Plymouth Rock.

SALES GIRL. *(laughing)* Oh, Miss Pilford. Miss Dale, shall I charge these to your account and have them delivered?

(SALES GIRL takes packages and garments from MARY.)

MARY. That would be lovely. Thank you.

SALES GIRL. *(sighs, looking at hat)* And I suppose this poor little orphan goes back to Millinery. *(Laughs. She exits stage left door.)*

MARY. After this I thought we'd look at slacks.

PAT. No. We're going to talk. What's wrong, Mary?

MARY. Nothing's wrong.

PAT. Quit stalling. I'll get it out of you.

MARY. Am I so transparent?

PAT. Like a silk stocking without a run. It's Frank, isn't it?

MARY. Yes, it's Frank. Pat, I really don't want to discuss it and certainly not here in Bullocks.

PAT. Mary, this is Pat, you know Pat, P-A-T, zany, warm hearted, bad dye job, your best friend.

MARY. I think Frank may be seeing another woman.

PAT. Anyone we know?

MARY. Oh yes. Marta Towers.

PAT. *(speechless)* Don't even…did you catch them *in flagrante delicto?*

MARY. What?

PAT. Did you catch them in the act? The Soviet version of the old ooh la la.

MARY. No, nothing like that. It's only a suspicion, mind you. But I'm scared, Pat. Frank's growing away from me. It's as if I hardly know him anymore.

PAT. What's your evidence?

MARY. Marta's convinced him to join her method acting class.

PAT. Mary, if you let him walk through those doors, you'll never see him again.

MARY. What can I do?

PAT. You're so helpless. How did you become a star? You must have some steel in your girdle.

MARY. He's moved out of the house. I can't very well throw myself in front of his car.

PAT. Then you'll have to follow him there.

MARY. I couldn't. He'd be furious.

PAT. Better angry now then divorced later. Don't you see, Mary, it's not Marta that he loves, it's what she stands for, high art and all that crap. If it was sex he was after, he'd be hot tailing it with some carhop with big bazooms, not some egg-headed pinko. Face it, girl, your enemy isn't pussy, it's Stanislavsky! Want me to play sidekick?

MARY. No, I must do this alone. If only I could be sure this was the right thing to do.

PAT. Trust Pat. How many times must I tell people, ideas are dangerous. Squash 'em!

MARY. Pat, you're so vehement.

PAT. Maybe it's just that…well I knew a woman once who loved a man, desperately. He too became infatuated with an idea and the little fool did nothing and lost him. Well enough of that malarkey. Hey, what do you say we look at them hats and get you a spiffy one for your entree into the academy of dramatic art.

MARY. Well perhaps there is method in your madness.

(She laughs.)

PAT. Shakespeare, ain't it? And who says we ain't highbrow.

(They link arms and exit through stage left door.)

(blackout)

Scene 5

*(That night. The administrative office of the Yetta Felson Acting School. **BARKER**, a heavyset man with a cigar is seated behind the desk, stage right. **R.G. BENSON**. an elegant director is seated in a swivel armchair smoking a pipe. **MITCHELL DRAKE**, standing at the downstage side of the desk is lighting his cigarette. and **BARKER**'s cigar as the lights come up. **MALCOLM** is pacing.)*

BARKER. Don't be a nervous Nellie, Malcolm.

MALCOLM. Mr. Barker, I wish you wouldn't speak to me like that.

BARKER. You're too sensitive. Sit down. I looked in on Yetta's class. Taggart's buying the whole megillah.

MITCHELL. Taggart's hooked on the method like a rug.

BARKER. *(snickering)* Actors and their craft.

R.G. La Felson most certainly has a messianic quality.

BARKER. I love the way this guy talks. Class all the way. Scene Study should be over any minute. Marta will bring Taggart to the office and before you can say "Charlie Chaplin," he'll be signed, sealed and delivered.

MALCOLM. You will be gentle with him? He's a very vulnerable kind of guy.

BARKER. What do you take me for, a bully? You hurt my feelings, Malcolm. I have a great respect for artists. What other organization can boast a famous New York playwright such as Mitchell Drake and an Oscar-winning film director like the great R.G. Benson.

R.G. You're most flattering, Mr. Barker.

BARKER. R.G., we would be greatly honored to display your Oscar here at the Felson school.

R.G. I wish I could comply but my aged mother has it prominently displayed in her den in Black Hills, South Dakota and I couldn't possibly...

BARKER. Are you refusing me?

R.G. I'm merely saying that...

MITCHELL. *(crudely)* Get this straight, Benson. We don't take too kindly being turned down by some Hollywood hack who can't keep his pecker out of every female child star on the lot.

R.G. I would be delighted to donate my Oscar.

BARKER. Donation accepted.

MARTA. *(offstage)* This way.

BARKER. Box up! Here they come.

> *(****FRANK**** and ****MARTA**** enter stage left door. ****MARTA**** is wearing a black strapless cocktail dress.)*

BARKER. Well, well, well Mr. Taggart. A great pleasure. I've so admired your work. It's almost like magic the way you can turn the most trivial formula picture into a penetrating character study. I'm Bertram Barker, the President of the Yetta Felson School.

FRANK. You're more than kind, Mr. Barker. Malcolm?

MALCOLM. I work part-time in the office. I hope you don't mind that I'm moonlighting.

FRANK. Of course not. I just sat in on the scene study class. Yetta Felson is a genius. Such insight. I'd love to meet her.

BARKER. In due time, my boy, in due time.

FRANK. *(passionately)* I can't wait to roll up my sleeves and get to work. I have so many demons needing to be released.

BARKER. Well, young man, just sign here on the dotted line and you can start releasin' them demons tomorrow night. *(He hands ****FRANK**** a sheath of papers.)*

FRANK. A thick contract. I suppose I should take it home and read it

MITCHELL. It's a standard acting school contract

MARTA. Darling, don't waste your time reading the fine print.

R.G. Most definitely migraine inducing.

MALCOLM. There's no harm in him taking it home overnight.

MITCHELL. Malcolm, stick to filing and light typing. Taggart, trust me, it's strictly standard stuff.

FRANK. Hell, why not. Where do I sign?

BARKER. At the bottom of the page here. All four copies. You'll be getting your card in three weeks.

(As FRANK *signs the contracts,* BARKER *gives a cynical wink to* MITCHELL.*)*

BARKER. Shall we have a drink toasting our new member?

*(*MALCOLM *passes out shot glasses.)*

FRANK. Thank you sir, but I think I'll pass.

BARKER. Drink. Drink. Have a snort. It's a crime to pass up good Russian vodka. I knew from the first second I saw him up on the screen he was one of us.

MITCHELL. We're in the presence of a true artist.

*(*FRANK *takes a shot, his hand betraying an alcoholic's tremor.)*

BARKER. That'a boy.

MITCHELL. Congratulations.

(All drink.)

MARTA. Welcome aboard, darling.

BARKER. Drake, you're the genius writer. Tell Frank more about our operations…I mean our artistic manifesto.

MITCHELL. To us, acting is more than just making faces. It's a way of looking at life. That's why we're making every effort to make message films that expose society's corruption. The kind of performance we develop here at the studio can be painful but as Spinoza says "pain and pleasure are merely transitions to a greater state of perfection." It's a revolutionary approach.

FRANK. *(in rapture)* Yes, yes, revolutionary.

BARKER. First we take over Hollywood and then the nation. Nostrovya!

ALL. *(except* FRANK*)* Nostrovya!

MALCOLM. *(enthusiastically)* After the revolution, sex roles will be undefined. We'll accept that we're all part male and female and that human nature is meant to be bisexual.

BARKER. Oh ho ho, wait just a minute. Don't get carried away, son. There ain't no place in the revolution for that kind of thinking.

MALCOLM. What do you mean? You told me when I joined the party, that you were all for sexual freedom.

BARKER. No siree, you weren't listening. I never said that. I meant free love between men and women.

MALCOLM. But I thought Marxism meant that all workers were one, all equal.

BARKER. That's right, kid. All equal and all normal. In the American communist society, all bedrooms will be monitored. Those who don't conform will be dragged into the light.

MALCOLM. I'm finally coming to my senses. What could I have been thinking of? You're not my friends. You people are dangerous.

MARTA. You're the one who's dangerous. You'd destroy the revolution with your decadence.

MITCHELL. Deviationist!

R.G. Trotskyite!

FRANK. Hey, wait just a minute. Malcolm was just saying…

MARTA. Shut up! Wrong thinkers must be weeded out and destroyed.

R.G. There can be only one voice and that belongs to the state. Hail Big Brother!

ALL. Hail Big Brother and Mother Russia!

MALCOLM. This has been most enlightening. I think it's time for me to leave. I'll have you know I'm ripping up my membership card.

MITCHELL. You insignificant worm. You think you can fight the party? Not a chance. We'll bury you.

R.G. What do you suppose you'll do for a job?

MALCOLM. I have a job with Frank Taggart.

BARKER. I happen to know your boss and you've just been fired.

FRANK. Hey, I never said...

BARKER. Shut up! *(to* MALCOLM*)* Kid, you'll never work in this town again.

MALCOLM. Then I'll move to another city. I'm Competent. I've got skills. There's always a position for a good hairdresser.

MARTA. You fool. After we start our whispering campaign, no first rate salon would ever hire you. Eventually they'll revoke your operator's license. Perhaps you could get a job as a hairburner in some flea-bitten perm parlor off the highway but even there, after a few weeks, your employer will receive a copy of your membership card. Then see how fast they'll snatch away your perm rods.

R.G. I'm afraid there's no place you can hide. No place to run.

MALCOLM. I'd rather take that chance. Dear Lord in heaven, forgive me for losing my faith.

MITCHELL. Can it with that Bible junk!

MALCOLM. Mother Mary, full of grace, how wrong I was to denounce my country, sweet land of liberty, of thee I sing...

MARTA. *(hands over her ears as if they were burning)* Shut up! Shut up! Shut up!

MALCOLM. God save us all. *(He runs out. Exit stage left door.)*

BARKER. Benson, follow him. The little twirp wouldn't dare sing to the FBI with all the dirt we've got on him. Still. I want you to monitor his every move. Marta. start the whispering campaign.

MARTA. *(whispering)* Yes sir.

R.G. I'll be on him. like a hound dog after a fox.

BARKER. Yeah, yeah, yeah, just beat it.

   *(*R.G. *exits stage left door.)*

FRANK. It's late. I should be going.

MITCHELL. You're not getting cold feet, are you?

FRANK. To be honest, I am. I signed up for a class in Stanislavsky's method, not a political organization.

BARKER. Oh you didn't, huh. *(picks up contract)* You should have read the fine print "I Frank Taggart, am hereby a loyal sworn member of the Communist party and dedicate my life to the downfall and destruction of the American way of life."

FRANK. You fat tub of lard, you conned me.

(He springs at **BARKER.** **MITCHELL** *belts him in the stomach.* **FRANK** *doubles over and sinks back into the chair.)*

MITCHELL. Should we have the goon squad toss him into the Pacific?

BARKER. No. I think Mr. Taggart has gotten that little demon out of his system. Eh, Nisowitz?

FRANK. How did you know that was my name?

MARTA. The party knows everything about you. We've got a dossier on Moishe Nisowitz three inches thick.

MITCHELL. We know where you came from and why you had to leave. I don't think the fan magazines would like to hear how the young Moishe Nisowitz killed his childhood buddy.

FRANK. It was an accident. Izzie and I were kayaking in the East River. We were horse playing as teenagers do and he hit himself over the head with an oar and fell into the river. It was an accident.

MITCHELL. The police would be very interested in hearing your side of the story since you ran away like a coward.

MARTA. Darling, it doesn't look good. My prediction is definitely twenty years to life.

FRANK. The studio would bail me out. They've got the top lawyers in…

BARKER. Forget it, Nisowitz, you're in a bind. Swear your loyalty to the party. Swear it!

MITCHELL. Swear it!

MARTA. Swear it!

FRANK. *(grabbing his head with both hands in torment)* I can't take anymore. Why are you browbeating me?

MITCHELL. *(scientifically)* He's cracking.

BARKER. We're your friends. Frankie. Not the government, not the studio. Just place your right hand on this here copy of Karl Marx and say "I swear loyalty to the Communist party."

*(From behind the file cabinet. we see **MARY** hiding. First we see her hat, then her eyes. She is wearing the silly hat the **SALES GIRL** carried in at Bullocks.)*

MITCHELL. We don't have all night, Nisowitz.

FRANK. *(painfully)* I swear…I swear loyalty to the Communist party.

*(**MARY**'s eyes nearly pop out.)*

BARKER. Let's get down to business. We must begin to implement our three step plan to take over the motion picture industry. Number one: All film scripts must promote the communist way of life. I see these films shot in a nice black and white. Number two: the termination of personal ambition. All starlets will be rounded up and shipped off to re-education camps. Number three and most important: the end of the star system. No person can be placed above the proletariat. All films will be ensemble productions with no star billing, no glamour wardrobe and definitely no special lighting or filters.

*(**MARY**'s eyes register total contempt.)*

Any star who defies the system will be eliminated.

*(**MARY** gasps.)*

What was that?

MARTA. It must be someone upstairs in the sense memory class.

BARKER. Taggart, this is where you come in. The symbol of capitalist Hollywood is the Arthur Freed musical unit over at Metro. It must be destroyed.

FRANK. But what can I do?

MITCHELL. Your wife is shooting a musical about Lady Godiva. We want you to spy on her. Use her to get all the dirt on the Freed unit, who's boffing who, which men are fairies, who's popping pills.

BARKER. We need you to get the dirt that women only discuss in the privacy of their homes.

MARTA. And you'll get plenty from that loud mouthed Pilford dame. She's been flapping her trap about me since I got off the train at Union Station.

(**MARY** *in disgust, gasps and forgets to duck down.* **MITCHELL** *sees her.*)

MITCHELL. Hey look!

BARKER. You get out here.

FRANK. Mary, what are you doing here?

MARY. I had to see for myself if my suspicions were true. This is far worse than I ever imagined.

MARTA. So the good little wife finally wakes up.

FRANK. Can it, Marta.

MARTA. I'm not afraid of her.

MARY. Marta, I feel very sorry for you.

MARTA. Sorry for me?

MARY. Because in your quest for love, you've allowed yourself to be manipulated into a world of corruption. Now that corruption is showing in your face and that's the kind of ugliness even the House of Westmore can't repair.

MARTA. She can't talk to me that way. Mr. Barker, do something.

MARY. Don't you see darling, that everything they're feeding you is a lie. All of these people are embittered failures who couldn't make it within the system so now they seek to destroy it. Look at Marta, spinning her wheels in B-movies. She didn't have what it takes to be a true star, beauty, glamour, drive. There always have been stars and there always will be. It's the reason one kitten stands out in a litter. It's part of the great cosmos around us. Politics come and go but the star system is eternal.

MARTA. *(viciously)* It's a lie! A lie! You're not an actress. There's no interior life behind your eyes. You have a dead face. Dead! Blank! Dead!

MARY. Come to your senses, darling. It's wrong. It's all wrong. Jamison has the car waiting for us around the block. Take me home, darling.

*(**FRANK** moves towards her.)*

BARKER. Trailing after the little woman. You're weak, Taggart, you're weak.

FRANK. But she's my wife.

BARKER. No wonder your audience laughs at your love scenes. Pathetic.

MITCHELL. Be a man. Grow some hair on your balls.

MARTA. Remember Izzie in the East River.

FRANK. *(tortured. makes up his mind)* Go home, Mary.

MARY. Frank!

FRANK. I told you to go home. This is where I belong.

MARY. I don't believe you. You've been brainwashed.

MITCHELL. You heard what the man said. Get lost.

FRANK. Yeah, beat it. Get out of here. If you thought you could lead me around on a leash, you were very much mistaken. I'm not one of your flunkies who jump at your every command.

MARY. Darling, what are you saying?

FRANK. I'm saying we're through. I'm not coming home again.

MARY. Say it so I'll believe it.

FRANK. Go home!

MARY. I don't believe you.

FRANK. Go home!

MARY. It's the party speaking. I want to hear from your own lips that you want me to leave.

FRANK. *(as loud as he can shout)* GO HOME!!!!

MARY. *(quietly)* Very well, I'll leave. Good luck

FRANK. You'll need it.

MARTA. Dead Face!

(MARY starts to exit but decides to prove to MARTA that she doesn't have a dead face. She proceeds to look wistfully, then hurt, then vengeful, then tormented. She sneers, curls her lip and generally gives MARTA every look that could kill. When she finishes this display of facial pyrotechnics, she matter-of-factly says:)

MARY. Good night. *(exits stage right)*

BARKER. She knows too much. Something must be done.

FRANK. What are you saying?

MITCHELL. Something must be done about Mary Dale.

BARKER. *(to FRANK)* And you're going to do it.

FRANK. *(panicked)* No! No! You can't ask me to do that. Please!

MARTA. Frank you wouldn't want us to tell the FBI that we've found Moishe Nisowitz. They're very anxious to know more about that nasty little crime which may or may not have been a murder. Either angle won't look good on your resume.

MITCHELL. Here's the situation, Taggart. Mary's life and we cover it up most efficiently or your previous crime is revealed and you're sent up the river on first degree murder. It's your choice.

BARKER. Quite a pickle you're in, Taggart. Quite a pickle.

FRANK. Please. There must be another way. Please. Please.

(The three communists close in on the pleading FRANK.)

(blackout)

END OF ACT I

ACT II

Scene 1

(The next morning at the studio. The set of "Godiva Was a Lady.")

*(**R.G. BENSON** enters stage right. **STAGEHANDS** set up **R.G.**'s directing chair and a klieg light. **RUDY**. the assistant director, enters with a clapboard. **MARY** enters dressed as a musical comedy Lady Godiva. with a long switch of hair attached to her short 1950s coiffure.)*

R.G. Mary, are you ready?

MARY. Yes, R.G.

R.G. Quiet please. We're ready to shoot.

(Bell rings.)

Lights! Camera! Rudy, slate it.

RUDY. *(snapping the clapboard)* "Godiva Was a Lady" Scene 23. Take 1.

R.G. Roll playback.

VOICEOVER. Roll film.

(Music starts.)

R.G. Action!

*(**MARY** begins lipsynching to playback. The song is a cheerful upbeat tune suitable for a musical about Lady Godiva. Midway through the number, she falters.)*

R.G. Are you all right?

MARY. I'm so sorry. I don't know what came over me.

R.G. Mary, dear, perhaps you should lie down.

MARY. No, no. I don't want to keep everyone waiting.

R.G. You're the most solid pro I've ever worked with. *(to the crew)* Everyone, break for ten!

MARY. You're awfully kind. I can see why every actress in town longs to work for you. *(She sits in the director's chair.)* Is there anything we can salvage from that last take?

R.G. Probably not. And not much from this morning either.

MARY. R,G., you should have told me if I was falling short.

R.G. There's nothing that we can't reshoot. But I am concerned by what I see in your eyes. You can't fool the camera. What's troubling you, Mary?

MARY. Don't you read the fan magazines? My life is perfect. The perfect career, the perfect house, the perfect marriage… *(She breaks down.)*

R.G. Mary, I like to think that I'm more than just your director. You do consider me a friend?

MARY. Oh, I do. I do. *(She clasps his hand.)* But there are things that I can't talk about. I run through every platitude and old chestnut, but they don't seem to make much sense any more.

R.G. I have faith in you, Mary. You're from good strong stock, with all the right values. You'll endure and survive.

MARY. Strange you should say that. I was brought up on the simple values taught to me by my grandmother who was taught by her grandmother that life could be beautiful. One married, had children, worked hard and made a profit. Now I find my every belief shattered and exposed to ridicule

R.G. Mary, you're tired. You've shot five pictures back to back.

MARY. Oh, I am tired. It's hard to sleep when you're living a nightmare.

R.G. Mary, I think I can help you. *(reaches in his pocket and takes out a vial of pills)* I'm going to give you these sleeping pills. Take one a night and you will find your restful sleep.

MARY. All in a little pill.

R.G. Promise me you won't be foolish and take too many.

MARY. I promise, Dr. Benson.

R.G. I have one other prescription. Lose yourself in work. Whatever your private hell is, use it in this role. Expose yourself. And be the great actress we know you can be.

MARY. Let's be honest, R.G., we both know I'm not really an actress. I've never appeared in a real role, in a real play. You can't call what I do, acting.

R.G. Mary Dale, you stop this at once! Do you hear me? If you want to be a real actress, then act! I've got a script that would be perfect for you. It's a serious drama that sends home a powerful message. It's a blistering indictment, never shirking from its ugly truths.

MARY. *(vulnerably)* You'd really want me?

R.G. What a challenge to reveal to the public a new Mary Dale, devoid of make-up.

*(**MARY**'s eyes pop open wide with alarm and suspicion.)*

Now mind you, it's not a star vehicle. It's an ensemble piece. It'll be shot in black and white on a very low budget. No glamorous wardrobe or flattering lighting, or fillers.

*(**MARY** listens to him with mounting horror. He's spouting the radical plans she overheard at the communist cell.)*

R.G. I see it intrigues you.

MARY. R.G., I've always meant to ask you, what is that marvelous cologne you wear?

R.G. Oh, it was given to me as a gift a long time ago. You can't even get it in this country. It's called "Moscow Breeze."

MARY. I believe I met a girl who wears the perfume.

R.G. Marta Towers. A lovely girl. Really unfair, the scandalous rumors that follow...

(**R.G.** *continues to talk but his dialogue is drowned out by cacophonous music and* **MARY**'s *thoughts.*)

MARY. *(voiceover)* He's in on it. Part of the conspiracy. A communist. They're everywhere.

(The music fades out. **MARY**'s *face instantly switches from hysteria to a calm facade.)*

R.G. Feeling any better, Mary?

MARY. Oh yes. Everything is much clearer now.

R.G. Shall we get back to work? Perhaps we can begin our new realism now and have the cameraman remove some of those filters.

MARY. Let's not be hasty.

R.G. *(laughs)* You're quite a gal, Mary. Quite a gal.

(He exits.)

*(***MARY*** returns to the set. the playback begins again and she stares at* **R.G.**, *his back to her, with great suspicion.)*

Scene 2

(A telephone booth in Los Angeles. **MALCOLM** *enters furtively. He goes into the phone booth, takes out a crumpled piece of paper and dials a number.)*

MALCOLM. Hello, is this the Chateau la Tress? Hello Eleanor. This Malcolm Levine. I was in the salon yesterday auditioning for Randy's chair. It was a nice surprise seeing such a classy beauty salon just off the highway...I had a lovely afternoon. You have such a friendly staff. You know, Eleanor, I was able to clear all my plans. I could start immediately... Oh really...

*(***MITCHELL DRAKE*** *enters and stops for a moment to light a cigarette.)*

But I thought you were so desperately understaffed... You know, Eleanor, I'm also great with perms...I don't want to put you on the spot but is there another reason why you don't want me. You can tell me. (***MALCOLM*** *notices* **MITCHELL** *and panics.)* Look Eleanor, I really can't talk...I have to... Yes, I...

*(***MALCOLM*** *hangs up abruptly. He pulls his collar up to hide his face and sneaks out of the phone booth and runs to avoid* **MITCHELL***.)*

Scene 3

(The Radio Station. **PAT PILFORD** *is standing before the mike.)*

PAT. Hey, this is a voice in the wilderness. Can anybody hear me? Is Mary Dale here yet?

TECHNICIAN. *(voiceover)* She's in the green room, Miss Pilford. All the guests have arrived. Could you give us something for a sound check?

PAT. *(with an exaggerated New York accent)* Soitenly.

*(*MITCHELL DRAKE *enters.)*

One, two, three, four. *(She sings to the tune of* Over the Rainbow.*)* Somewhere over my boobies, Bluebirds crapped. That's it, folks. Anymore of Aunt Patty's ditties you pay for.

MITCHELL. *(applauds her)* The same old Pat. The funniest gal in the world. You really ought to visit my psychiatrist-friend, Dr. Hans Mueller. His theory "Dirty jokes as a sexual deterrent" fits you like Dotty Lamour's sarong.

PAT. I'd like to know how you got in here.

MITCHELL. Doors have a way of opening for me.

PAT. If you're here for the broadcast, we won't be starting for several minutes.

MITCHELL. You can knock off the great lady schtick. I told you I'd be seeing you.

PAT. You really are the most contemptible…

MITCHELL. I said knock it off.

PAT. And now?

MITCHELL. That's better. *(picks up her hand)* Yes, you had beautiful hands. I'd forgotten that. *(kisses her fingers)*

PAT. *(afraid she'll give in)* Please, Mitch, please don't do that.

MITCHELL. Why? Because you'll forget you're the slapstick Statue of Liberty. You miss me, don't you?

PAT. I miss the fellow who wasn't so twisted with hate.

MITCHELL. Yes, I hate. I hate those who would deny me my right to build a better world.

PAT. And I hate those that seek to destroy everything I hold sacred. But you don't frighten me, Mitch. Your automatons can infiltrate all of our industries but the American people will never capitulate their freedoms.

MITCHELL. You really believe this crap you dish out on the radio every week.

PAT. Of course I do.

MITCHELL. That's too bad because you're about to switch sides.

PAT. You're out of your mind.

MITCHELL. No, but very lucky. I have in my possession some entertaining photographs taken fifteen years ago of a nubile Pat Pilford, America's own, performing some of the most disgusting, degrading sexual acts imaginable.

PAT. Acts you made me do.

MITCHELL. And you loved every minute of it.

PAT. What are you planning to do with those photos?

MITCHELL. I could be persuaded to lock them away forever. If and I say *if,* you cooperate with the party.

PAT. You really are out of your mind. Besides no publication would ever print such filth.

MITCHELL. We wouldn't need to publish them. They'd be distributed by our network of followers to every town and city in the old U.S. of A. And with that memorable mug of yours, there would be no doubt as to the frisky model's identity.

(PAT *breaks down in tears.*)

MITCHELL. I hate seeing you cry, Pat.

(*He tries to hand her his handkerchief. She flinches.*)

You had to be stopped·

PAT. *(with rising egomania)* I suppose this order came directly from party headquarters in Moscow.

MITCHELL. Don't flatter yourself. I have a creative mind. I have after all, won a Pulitzer Prize. I can certainly figure out how to shut up one gabby comedienne.

PAT. All right. You've silenced my voice. Now get out of here.

MITCHELL. We're not quite finished yet. You're going to fire your writing staff.

PAT. But why? They're the best gag men in the business.

MITCHELL. You're all ready going to be gagged, baby. The party has new writers for you and will deliver you a polished script every week, starting with this one. *(He hands her a script.)*

PAT. I'd never read this garbage. You won't make me a commie tool.

MITCHELL. Remember the night you said "cheeze."

PAT. I'm a famous conservative. The public will never believe I'd turn around so completely.

MITCHELL. It'll be subtle at first. A gradual coming to your senses. You better go over your lines. We want you to be convincing. Oh, look, you've got a nice big studio audience coming in ready to listen to good old Pat. See ya, kid.

(As MITCHELL exits. MARY enters carrying her script.)

MITCHELL. Hello Mary.

MARY. Mr. Drake, I have nothing to say to you.

MITCHELL. If only Gogol could have written about you. So lovely and so absurd.

MARY. *(smugly)* Who's this Mr. Gogol? A fellow traveler?

(She walks past him to PAT. MITCHELL shakes his head in disbelief and exits.)

MARY. Pat darling. I'm sorry I'm late. What was Mitchell Drake doing here?

PAT. Was that Mitchell Drake? I've never met him.

MARY. What's wrong, Pat? You're as white as this paper.

PAT. I always get the willies. We should be on the air any

minute.

MARY. Pat, you won't believe what I've been through. What I've seen, what I've heard.

PAT. Shhhhh, we can't talk now.

MARY. I know, we can't…it's just that…Pat, I'm in the middle of a communist conspiracy. Frank, Marta, R.G. Benson, Mitchell Drake. I need your help. You're so strong. Tell me what to do.

PAT. *(urgently)* Do nothing.

MARY. What?

PAT. Do nothing. You don't know these people. How far they'll go.

MARY. That's so unlike you.

PAT. You wanted my advice. Well, that's it. Whatever happens, keep silent.

DIRECTOR. *(voiceover)* Ladies, we'll be starling in thirty seconds.

MARY. Pat, something's bothering you. What is it?

PAT. I told you nothing's wrong.

MARY. You're trembling.

PAT. *(sharply)* Mary, I'm about to do a show. Be a professional and stop wasting my time with your silly paranoia.

DIRECTOR. *(voiceover)* Fifteen seconds to air.

PAT. Oh Mary, the script has been rewritten somewhat. Just a few of my lines. Nothing major. It doesn't affect you.

DIRECTOR. *(voiceover)* Five, four, three, two.

PAT. Here we go.

ANNOUNCER. *(voiceover)* The Veedol Motor Oil Program with Pat Pilford.

(applause/music)

Makers of Veedol Motor Oil, found wherever fine cars travel, present Miss Show Business, Pat Pilford. With Emmaline Crane, Jimmy Stall and special guest stars Mary Dale, Olson and Johnson, Helen Traubel, the

Ames Brothers, Yours truly Bill Simmons and Victor Arnold and his Chiffon Orchestra. And now your fabulous femm-cee, Pat Pilford.

PAT. *(reading from the new script)* Welcome comrades.

*(**MARY** is startled but tries to ignore it.)*

For the sake of variety, I'd like to skip my usual opening and bring out my special guest, lovely film star, Mary Dale. Besides, I know I've been boring you to tears these past months with my idiotic red baiting. I don't know a fool thing about politics. Please ignore anything I may have said. Believe me, I was wrong, wrong, wrong! Mary, come on out here. Mary Dale.

(applause)

How are ya, darlin'?

MARY. *(reading from her script)* Tip top. I'm so glad we could finally get together on your show. Pat, you look marvelous, but if you get any blonder, the studio won't need light bulbs.

PAT. *(reading from the new script)* Interesting that you should mention that, dear. I've decided today to let my hair go back to its natural mousey brown color. I'm beginning to realize that hair dye and make-up are simply capitalist tools that blind women to ideological realities.

MARY. *(reading her script. very perplexed)* Thank you, Pat. I loved making that picture. When are we going to do one together? I'm dying to do a wild slapstick comedy but it will be in my contract that I throw the pies.

PAT. That would be such a waste of good food. Food that could be divided equally among the working class. The more I think about it, darling, bakers should unite and deny the rich their decadent cakes and cookies.

MARY. *(realizing that none of her lines make sense in this context)* I love this dress too. It's a Don Loper original.

PAT. Mary, if you don't mind, I'd like to take this moment to tell my listeners what exactly is going on in this country. My dear comrades, we are in the grip of a...

(**MARY** *looks at* **PAT** *aghast as* **PAT** *reads her communist propaganda. Threatening music overpowers* **PAT** *so we can no longer hear her. Over the music,* **MARY**'*s thoughts are heard.*)

MARY. *(voiceover)* This can't be real. Not Pat. She couldn't be one of them. All of them pinkos, all of them red.

(*The music fades out.*)

PAT. My, it feels good getting that off my chest. Now Mary, tell us about...

(**MARY** *starts to move away from the mike.*)

Mary, come a little closer, dear. We're losing you.

MARY. *(distraught)* I'm sorry. I forgot something...I...I... I've got to run. (**MARY** *runs out of the studio.*)

PAT. Mary!

Scene 4

(The beach house. A short time later. FRANK is waiting for her. He's reading a book. A small gift box is on the coffee table next to him. MARY enters stage right door, holding her purse.)

MARY. Frank, you're home.

FRANK. *(puts the book on the coffee table open)* I've been here for hours, waiting, hoping you'd come back soon.

MARY. *(puts her purse down)* You look tired.

FRANK. Please take me back, Mary. I'm so miserable. How could I have been such a fool to think what they had to offer was real. It was all an illusion.

MARY. Marta Towers is hardly an illusion.

FRANK. I hate her. I wish she were dead. Believe me, Mary, I was never unfaithful. I couldn't go through with it. I love you so.

MARY. *(very confused)* Frank, I'd like to believe that. *(giving in)* Oh darling, come here. *(They embrace.)* How can two people who love each other as we do be so silly.

FRANK. Is it possible for you to forgive me? They don't come lower than me.

MARY. *(emotionally)* Of course I forgive you. You're my husband. I made a vow.

FRANK. *(passionately)* It's this town. Come away with me, Mary. New York, London, anywhere.

MARY. I will darling. Anywhere. My poor lost boy.

FRANK. It's going to be different. I'm going to change. I will. Starting tonight.

MARY. Tonight?

FRANK. Do you smell something cooking?

MARY. Yes.

FRANK. It's called dinner. And I'm cooking it myself. I gave Selina and all the servants the night off. Wanted you all to myself. I have so much to make up to you.

MARY. *(playfully)* You were awfully confident that I'd forgive you.

FRANK. I wasn't confident. I got on my knees and prayed.

MARY. Did you, Frank? And to what God?

FRANK. *Your* Lord, Mary. Now, Madame, if you'll excuse me, I must return to the kitchen to check up on my sauce reductions. *(He clicks his heels like a butler.)*

MARY. *(laughing)* Oh my. Taggart, you may go.

FRANK. Yes, mum. *(He exits stage left door.)*

MARY. *(lighting up a cigarette)* They may all be communists but not my husband. Not my Frank. *(calling to the kitchen)* Will we be eating soon, darling?

FRANK. I can't hear you, dear.

MARY. *(calling offstage)* How soon will we be eating? Do I have time to call my aunt in Indiana?

FRANK. *(offstage)* Darling, I'm sorry I can't understand you. I'll be right out.

MARY. *(Laughs. Sits in the chair stage right and picks up phone on the stage right level to dial.)* Hello... Hello... That's odd.

FRANK. *(enters stage left door)* Darling, what is it you asked me?

MARY. The telephone's dead. I can't even get an operator.

FRANK. Give it to me. *(He takes the phone.)* You're right. Dead as my last picture. I'll go next door and report it on the Stewart's line.

MARY. No, no, no. You're busy cooking. I suppose for ten hours we could do without the blasted telephone. It'll be a pleasure.

FRANK. You're so pretty. *(He kisses her forehead. Exits stage left door.)*

MARY. This is our home that we built together. A mighty fortress. But does it have to be such a mess? Why must we have so many books? They do collect dust. *(She crosses to coffee table and picks up book.)* Cousin Bette by Balzac. Oh my. *(She opens it where **FRANK** left the marker.)*

Shame on him. Scribbling in the margin. "...poisoned by a prick of a needle in the clasp of her necklace." How ghastly. *(She closes book and puts it down on the coffee table.)* Give me Fanny Hearst any day. *(She picks up jewelry box from coffee table.)* What's this? *(She opens box.)* Oh, how lovely.

(She takes necklace out of box, crosses right and holds necklace up. Her face is away from the audience. Sound cue. She turns towards the audience, her face a mask of sudden fear and terror.)

FRANK. *(enters stage left door)* Oh, you found it. I wanted to surprise you with it after dinner. Every pearl so perfect and exactly alike. Almost mesmerizing. Exquisite, aren't they?

MARY. *(trying to compose herself)* Yes, they are, rather.

FRANK. They'll be even more perfect once they're around your neck.

(He tries to stroke her neck, she moves away.)

You pulled away.

MARY. Did I?

FRANK. I think we should put these on you now. Get a special preview.

MARY. No, I don't think so.

FRANK. Why don't you want to put them on, Mary?

MARY. Is there a reason why I shouldn't put them on?

FRANK. None in the world. They were specially designed for you.

MARY. That's what I thought.

FRANK. I can put them on for you. It's a simple clasp. *(He moves closer to her.)* Why are you moving away, Mary?

MARY. Darling, I really don't want to put them on. Please dear. Put them down.

FRANK. *(with a quiet urgency)* I can't, Mary. I have to do this. I don't want to. They've made me. They're bigger than we are. We can't fight 'em. This is the way it has to end. Please, darling, don't fight me.

MARY. There must be another way. You love me. You must have loved me once. Please, Frank, it's me, Mary.

FRANK! Don't. Don't.

*(***FRANK*** *grabs her. She tries to fight him off. She bites his hand but he continues to try to put the necklace around her neck. In their struggle, he drops the necklace and finally grabs her around the throat and starts to strangle her. When she appears to be on the brink of death,* ***FRANK*** *suddenly wakes up and realizes he's about to murder his beloved wife. He breaks away in horror.)*

FRANK. What am I doing? What have I become?

*(***FRANK*** *staggers and runs out. He exits stage right door.* ***MARY*** *is panting for breath. The cacophonous music starts again and* ***MARY*** *in her hysteria hears threatening voices.)*

MARY. *(voiceover)* Frank, what's happened to us?

FRANK. *(voiceover)* We can't fight 'em. This is the way it has to end.

PAT. *(voiceover)* Whatever happens, keep silent.

MARTA. *(voiceover)* So the good little wife finally wakes up.

BARKER. *(voiceover)* Stars who defy the system will be eliminated.

MARY. Stop! Stop!

R.G. *(voiceover)* It's called "Moscow Breeze."

FRANK. *(voiceover)* We can't fight 'em. *(echoes over and over)*

MITCHELL. *(voiceover)* Grow some hair on your balls!

PAT. *(voiceover)* Keep silent! *(echoes over and over)*

MARY. *(Collapses on the steps. Hysterical.)* Trapped. Desperate. In a trap. No exit...No exit

*(***MARY*** *runs over to find her purse. She rummages through it until she finds the vial of pills that* **R.G.** *gave her at the studio. She empties the pills into her hand and tosses them into her mouth. She then grabs the bottle of*

whiskey off the bar tray and chases down the pills with liquor. She stumbles and staggers to center stage, the pills kicking in. The music underscoring her hysteria reaches a pitch of dissonance and the lighting becomes distorted and full of swirling shapes. At last she collapses on the ground unconscious. The music turns dreamlike and the lighting covers everything with a golden hue. Two young **PAGES** *in medieval garb enter with gold banners. They place the banners above the two doorways stage right and stage left and exit.* **MARTA** *enters stage right dressed in medieval costume. In* **MARY**'s *dream. she is* **LADY PRUDWEN**, *lady-in-waiting to* **LADY GODIVA**. *She enters carrying a voluminous gold robe and cone-like medieval headdress.* **MARY** *rises in her dream confounded by the spectacle before her.)*

LADY PRUDWEN. *(dressing* **MARY** *in the gold robe and headdress)* Milady Godiva, we must make haste and dress you in your ceremonial robes. The very same robes you wore to last years Academy Awards governors ball.

MARY. But I'm not Lady Godiva!

LADY PRUDWEN. Shhh, Milady.

*(***PAGES** *cross downstage steps and strike props. both side units, and flip in stage right chair. Settee remains.)*

(Enter stage left: **ARNOLPH** *[***MITCHELL***]*, **BALDRIC** *[***BARKER***]*, & **LEOFRIC** *[***FRANK***] all in medieval costume.)*

ARNOLPH. The king must die! He shall ride to the cathedral to hear his Sunday mass and there upon the Cathedral steps, he shall meet his assassin's sword.

BALDRIC. And by the following morn you, Leofric, will be crowned King of all England.

LEOFRIC. *(panicked)* But good sirs, the people do love King Edward. They will not be pleased to see him replaced.

BALDRIC. *(sneering)* The people! What do the people know?

ARNOLPH. The peasants are cow-like in their ignorance. They shall be taxed heavily and their gold will fill our coffers.

LEOFRIC. *(to the men)* I cannot in good faith be a part of this treason.

ARNOLPH. Be a man. Grow some hair on thy fertile orbs.

MARY. *(joining the scene)* Frank, don't listen to them!

LEOFRIC. I can't fight 'em, Godiva. I can't fight 'em.

MARY. I'm not Lady Godiva. That's a role that I play. I'm Mary Dale Taggart. No, that's not me. I'm Mary Dale. No, that's my stage name. I'm Mary Louise Hoffstetter.

PRUDWEN. She babbles. Leofric, tis your destiny to be king and I to be your queen.

*(She caresses and kisses him. **MARY** is shocked.)*

FRANK. *(trying to fight her off)* But I love Godiva.

(They continue to kiss.)

MARY. *(in horror)* I've got to get out of here.

*(**MALCOLM** enters stage left as **THOMAS**, a monk.)*

THOMAS. Shall I hear your confession, Lady Godiva?

MARY. Yes, this is my confession. I'm not Lady Godiva. I'm a movie star and a homemaker. And I can prove it. I have a parking place on the MGM lot.

(All laugh.)

ARNOLPH. And where do we find this mythical spot?

MARY. It's called Culver City.

BALDRIC. She's mad.

MARY. I want to send a telegram, I mean a carrier pigeon to Dore Schary. He's the head of the studio. That's Dore Schary. S-C-H-A-R-Y.

LADY PRUDWEN. She's as mad as the poor Thane of Cawdor's late wife, Irma.

(All laugh. Smoke.)

MARY. I am not mad. *(to **FRANK** in classical Shakespearean tones)* Shrive me sir, slubber not this calamitous venture. Tho I may be but a croff and woosel, enfranchised to a clog, I possess by Circe's cup, a wisdom not to be dismissed like some cankered malt horse drudge. Nay! Swinge me soundly for I must clagger thee as would Judas' daughter. My heart cleaved with the blind bow boy's butt shaft and enscrolled with a Tyrian throstle!

(PAGES enter to strike banners.)

ARNOLPH. She speaks as a traitor! Send her to the tower for execution!

BALDRIC. Her head must be stricken from her body!

THOMAS. Heretic!

LADY PRUDWEN. Put her on the rack!

FRANK. No! Please! Don't!

ARNOLPH.. Seize her!

(All exit but MARY. PAGES strike banners.)

MARY. *(sobbing)* Pat, where arc you when I need you so desperately. Pat!

(PAT enters stage left door. She is dressed as a court jester, except for fishnet stockings and spike heels.)

PAT. Sweetie pie , I can't chat, I'm so late. I'm emceeing an execution. Some dame is losing her head.

MARY. That dame is me!

PAT. Then be a pro and march thee hither. You don't want to be tardy for your own execution.

MARY. Pat, please–

PAT. Honey, I'll meet you at the chopping block. I've gotta go over my material. Where are my writers? *(She exits stage left door.)*

MARY. There's no escape! I must throw myself into the moat! Farewell, my beloved. *(She exits stage right.)*

(The ghost of MARY's GRANNY LOU enters stage right door. GRANNY LOU is a simple farm woman, gentle but firm, holding a dish towel.)

GRANNY LOU. Mary-Godiva, don't you go near that water. You come over here... That's right, child, it's me.

Granny Lou. You're looking at my hair. It's not white anymore. The minute you get here, your hair goes back to its old color. Pretty isn't it. *(She sits on settee.)* Dear one, I wish I could invite you inside but it's not your time yet. I'm afraid I've gotta keep you on the other side of this screen door. There's a whole slew of us in the parlor, all watching over you. Maudie, Aunt Olive. We sure do love you. But honey, we're a bit disappointed, seeing you giving up like that. We know you've got that Hoffstetter gumption in you. The same gumption that your ancestors had in settling this vast and glorious land. Now use it, honey. Save yourself and save your husband. He's not a bad man, just so very scared. Save him, darlin'. One little person can make a difference. Sometimes a body has to do somethin'—oh, do somethin' crazy-like to make people stand up and take notice. You'll know what it is, honey. We don't need to tell you. My dear one. You shall prevail. You shall prevail.

*(***GRANNY LOU*** exits.)*

*(***PAGES*** enter, strike settee. ***THOMAS*** enters.)*

THOMAS. Look out the window! The Lady Godiva is riding naked through the streets of Coventry! All the peasants are covering their eyes. None will gaze upon her nakedness. Oh, my eyes. My eyes. They burn with pain. Oh, the agony. I can't see. I've gone blind! Blind! History shall know me as Peeping Tom. *(He exits.)*

*(From behind a scrim we see ***LADY GODIVA*** [***MARY***] riding naked upon her steed as offstage voices cheer. Fade to black.)*

GRANNY LOU. *(voiceover)* One person can make a difference. But sometimes you gotta do something crazy-like to make people stand up and take notice. You can't defeat the people. Not the real people. Not God's children. They always come to their senses. The truth shall prevail. The truth shall prevail...

Scene 5

(The hospital. **MARY** *is lying in a hospital bed, unconscious.* **FRANK** *by her side, worried. On the stage left level lies a Bible.)*

MARY. *(murmuring)* The truth shall prevail. The truth shall prevail.

FRANK. Come back to me, Mary. Please don't die.

*(**MARY** opens her eyes.)*

FRANK. Mary? Mary?

MARY. Am I naked?

FRANK. No, my darling. You're alive. You've come back.

MARY. Am I in a hospital? Have I gone mad?

FRANK. You tried to kill yourself and it was all my fault.

MARY. Yes, you tried to murder me. That was no dream.

FRANK. There's so much to explain.

MARY. Tell me now. The truth.

FRANK. The communist party found out I'd accidentally killed my childhood friend. They threatened to expose me unless I... Unless I murdered you. It was as if they hypnotized me. I should have killed myself.

MARY. No, Frank, that's the coward's way out.

FRANK. I can never atone for what I did to you. Mary, you'll never see me again.

MARY. No, Frank, that's not the answer either. I want to save our marriage.

FRANK. You would do that?

MARY. There's good inside you. I'd be willing to nurture it if you are.

FRANK. I've given up drinking. Last night, I poured all the booze down the sink.

MARY. Last time you told me you prayed. That was a falsehood. This time, I must ask you to pray before me. Hand me that Bible, Frank.

(He gives her Bible.)

Kneel. Kiss the Bible.

FRANK. Lord, please help me.

MARY. Forgive us our trespasses as we forgive those who trespass against us. Lead us not into temptation but deliver us from evil.

PAT. *(enters stage left door)* Mary, you're yourself again.

FRANK. *(to MARY)* My beautiful one.

PAT. Mary, the last time I saw you at the radio station. It was so hideous.

FRANK. Tell the truth, Pat. Tell us why you're suddenly spouting the party line.

PAT. I can't. You mustn't ask me that.

MARY. Then I want you to leave.

PAT. *(horrified)* Mary …

MARY. I want you out of here. This is my party line. No communists are welcome in this room.

PAT. *(crying)* Please don't throw me out. I'm so alone.

MARY. I mean it, Pat. I'm not afraid anymore. *(listens to herself)* "I'm not afraid." "I'm not afraid." *(with great strength)* I'm not afraid.

PAT. *(in awe)* Mary, what's come over you?

MARY. I never believed that dreams could change one but mine has. While I was in the coma, I journeyed to another world and what I saw there has given me new hope. *(with great intensity)* For the last time I demand to know, are you now or have you ever been a member of the communist party?!

PAT. *(breaks down)* NO, no, no, no, no. I hate the communists. I'd like to see them all exterminated. It's Mitchell Drake… He's blackmailing me.

FRANK. What's he got on you?

PAT. Years ago in New York, I was very much in love with the son of a bitch. Love. Whoever thought love could be a dirty word. I was obsessed with him. I was no longer a woman of achievement, but a thing. I abandoned all sense of decency. I was in his thrall. And always that penis staring at me, taunting me! Mocking me! One night he got me drunk and took photos of me performing some of the most repugnant acts a woman could do.

MARY. *(with genuine interest)* For instance?

PAT. To even tell you would be to insult you. Now he intends to distribute them nationally unless I remain a commie tool.

MARY. Then we must find the negatives.

PAT. *(vulnerably)* We?

MARY. Friend, we're in this together.

PAT. *(sobbing)* Oh Mary, it's been so awful.

MARY. They must be tucked away somewhere in the bowels of the Yetta Felson Studio. Girl, we go there tonight.

FRANK. You mustn't. It's too dangerous. Don't forget Mary that they want you murdered. They tried to get me to do it, the monsters.

PAT. What?

FRANK. They think Mary knows too much.

MARY. I overheard their plot to destroy the Freed Unit.

PAT. Over my dead body.

FRANK. I'll get those negatives for you.

MALCOLM. *(enters stage left door furtively)* Please, may I come in?

MARY. Malcolm, where've you been? I was out of my mind with worry. You left with my fine washables still in the sink.

MALCOLM. I've been many places but they follow me everywhere.

MARY. Who Malcolm?

MALCOLM. The party. I thought I could break away but they were right. There's no dark corner to hide in.

MARY. Stop this Malcolm and tell us everything.

MALCOLM. No, Mrs. Taggart, you were the only one who was ever nice to me in this whole stinkin' town.

PAT. How did it all go wrong?

MALCOLM. I came here from Secaucus, New Jersey, an idealistic young cosmetologist with a dream. Hungry to change the world and invent a new form of hair weave. The party promised to fight for tolerance for my people and supply me with human hair. It was all a sham.

FRANK. You're young. You've got your whole life ahead of you.

MALCOLM. I gave that up the day I walked into that building on Sunset. I just wanted to say goodbye. *(slightly mad)* This is a lovely hospital room, so high above the ground. The fifth floor, isn't it? I guess I finally made it to the top.

FRANK. Malcolm, what are you thinking of?

MALCOLM. The end, Frank, the end.

(MALCOLM runs off stage right. We hear him jump out the window. The glass breaking, the body crashing to the pavement, passersby screaming below.)

PAT. *(covering her face)* Horrible! Horrible!

MARY. Dear sweet Malcolm.

FRANK. Poor little guy.

MARY. *(with great compassion)* I suppose in a way it was the only end for Malcolm. He lived with such sorrow all his life, existing in that bizarre lonely netherworld of half-men.

FRANK. *(sensitively)* Perhaps then it is best this way.

MARY. But not for you Frank or you Pat. Lady Godiva defied her world and succeeded. And dag gummit, so will I!

(blackout)

Scene 6

(That night. The office of the Yetta Felson Studio. **FRANK** *is revealed at the desk rummaging through drawers.)*

*(***MARTA*** *Enters stage left door.)*

MARTA. Frank, what are you doing here?

FRANK. I wanted to leave a note for Barker. I was looking for a pencil.

MARTA. I don't believe you. You're indicating. The subtext is you're searching for something that you believe is hidden in that desk.

(We hear a man screaming in agony.)

FRANK. What's that?

MARTA. Jeff Patterson's working on a scene from *Life With Father*. You know you let us down. Yesterday, you were supposed to start scene study class and then kill your wife. You did neither. Not a good political move, darling.

FRANK. What if I told you I was sick and tired of political moves.

MARTA. All art is political.

FRANK. What if I told you Abbott and Costello are looking downright attractive.

MARTA. Frank, you're still not giving us one hundred percent. You need a private session with Yetta Felson. Your ideology needs some serious reinforcing. Come along, junior.

*(***MARTA*** *and* ***FRANK*** *exit stage left door.* ***MARY*** *and* ***PAT*** *enter stage right door from behind the curtain.)*

MARY. And to think I invited that creature into my home. Pat, you take the desk and I'll take the file cabinet.

(They open drawers and look through them.)

PAT. *(opens a file)* Hey look, Mary.

*(***MARY*** *crosses to her.)*

A list of the student body. It's certainly an impressive star roster and not an ounce of glamour in the lot of them.

MARY. Give it to me, dear. You never know when it might come in handy. *(puts roster in her purse and returns to file cabinet)* Pat, I think I may have stumbled onto something.

PAT. What is it, Mary?

MARY. A file marked "Project Pilford." Do I dare open it?

PAT. Go ahead.

MARY. *(Opens file and sees photos. Gasps.)* Ah! Oh! Ah!

PAT. Remember I did a contortionist act in Vaudeville. Are the negatives in there?

MARY. Everything's here. Now let's amscray before the ams-hay get back.

(MITCHELL enters.)

MITCHELL. Well, well, well, if it isn't Nancy Drew and her friend, Kama Sutra. You girls interested in signing up for a course in the method?

MARY. I have my own method. "Learn your lines and don't bump into the furniture."

MITCHELL. Find what you were looking for?

PAT. Yes, we have. Negatives included. You can tell your writers they can go on permanent coffee break.

(Laughs and takes out a sealed envelope from his pocket. While he talks he opens the letter with a letter opener from the desk.)

MITCHELL. You two ladies think you've got this problem all wrapped up. You found the dirty pictures. Well, what about the blue movie. I have in this envelope a document listing the contents of a Swiss safe deposit box including one sixteen millimeter pornographic home movie starring Pat Pilford.

(MARY looks at PAT in disbelief.)

PAT. *(At the end of her rope.)* HE MADE ME!!! Damn you Mitchell. Damn you to hell!

MITCHELL. *(laughing)* You can't win, Pat. You just never know where to draw the line. *(puts letter opener back on desk)* Mary, I'm touched by your devotion to your naughty friend. I wonder how far you'd go to save her from exposure. I might be willing to forget about this list provided you two join me in a sexy partouze once a week at a hotel of my choice.

(PAT in her hysteria, grabs the letter opened from the desk and stabs MITCHELL. He writhes in agony and falls down dead. PAT stands over him in dumb shock.)

MARY. Thank you, Pat. He deserved to die. *(rushes to PAT's side and holds her)* Darling, don't you worry about a thing. We're going to hire you the best shingle in town and you're going to beat this rap. Remember, dear, I was a witness.

(MARTA and FRANK enter. MARTA sees MITCHELL's dead body and screams. She rushes to the body.)

MARTA. You idiots! You blithering idiots. You've murdered one of the theatres' finest writers.

MARY. Now he belongs to the ages.

FRANK. *(joining MARY)* Mary, are you all right?

MARY. I'm fine, darling but we must get Pat out of here.

(BARKER enters followed by R.G. BENSON.)

BARKER. We heard screaming. What's going on? *(Sees MITCHELL's body. To MARTA:)* Is he dead?

MARTA. Yes, Mr. Barker. Pilford stabbed him.

MARY. I wish I had done it.

FRANK. That makes us a trio.

BARKER. You three are in a heap o'trouble. The list of possible indictments boggles the mind. Taggart, you've been a thorn in my side since day one. I have goon squads to take care of the likes of you. Marta, call in Vladimir. It's time to lance these carbunkles.

R.G. For once I must contradict you, Mr. Barker.

BARKER. Butt out, windbag.

R.G. Barker, this is one time you may want to listen. I realize you've dismissed me as simply one of your many artistic stooges but I must inform you that I'm more than that. *(lifts his jacket revealing a badge)* In fact. I've been placed here as an undercover agent by the FBI. How am I doing, Mary?

MARY. Aces, R.G.

PAT. Mary, did you know R.G. was a government agent?

MARY. I figured it out this morning. I knew in my heart that a great woman's director couldn't be red.

BARKER. I commend you on your performance, Benson. Highly polished. Yes. You had me quite fooled. Well, well, well.

(BARKER makes an awkward dash to the exit. FRANK tries to block him. BARKER grabs him and pushes him aside.)

BARKER. Out of my way, cretin! *(BARKER dashes out.)*

FRANK. He got away. Dammit, he got away.

MARY. Don't you worry. Mr. Hoover has men surrounding the building. The fat man won't get far.

FRANK. How do you know there are men outside?

R.G. Show them your badge, Mary. I appointed our girl an honorary G-man just a few hours ago.

(MARY pulls back her coat and flashes her badge.)

MARY. My new favorite piece of jewelry.

(A severe-looking OLD LADY enters. She speaks in a vaguely European accent.)

OLD LADY. Look at this office. I have never seen such a mess.

MARY. I should say so. You're not much of a cleaning lady. This whole school should be fumigated.

OLD LADY. My dear, I am not the cleaning lady. I am Yetta Felson.

MARY. Well, Miss Felson, without even mentioning your communist activities, I think you're doing American actors a dreadful disservice encouraging them to wallow in self-indulgence and disregarding every tenet of discipline and professionalism.

YETTA. One moment, my dear. First of all, I am not a communist. I am also an agent with the FBI. The United States government financed the Felson Studios as a front to ensnare communists in the film industry. Furthermore, I am sick to death of the Stanislavsky method. I've just signed to play the grandmother in the new Red Skelton picture.

MARY. R.G., you must keep me abreast.

MARTA. *(fiercely)* Comrade Felson, you have betrayed the Moscow Art Theatre.

MARY. My dear, I'd suggest you not fling accusations. R. G., may I?

R.G. Mary, she's all yours.

MARY. Ever since we first met at the *Young Man With A Horn* premiere, I found it curious your extreme aversion to signing autographs.

MARTA. There's nothing curious about that. Autograph collecting is a capitalist fetish encouraged to separate artists from the people.

MARY. A rudimentary phone call to the girls in the studio contract department revealed that even those documents were signed by proxy.

R.G. We were both left wondering where we could find your signature.

MARY. Certainly not in cement at Graumanns. No, it was I who finally discovered your Jane Hancock on this postcard from Tijuana. It perfectly matches the signature of one Olga Shumsky, a soviet agent of the KGB. The message itself was also a tip-off. "Having a great time but wish I was in Odessa."

MARTA. You're a liar! It's a frame-up.

MARY. No, Miss Shumsky. It is you who have created an identity built on lies. The real Marta Towers was a lovely, aspiring young actress who was found murdered on a lonely dirt road outside Tijuana. We have also located Dr. Leon Beidemann who performed extensive plastic surgery on you, enabling the dog-faced, moustached, piano-legged Olga Shumsky to successfully break into American show business. I charge you with the murder of Marta Towers.

MARTA. *(violently)* Yes! I am Commissar Olga Shumsky! And yes, I killed Marta Towers, the simpering little fool. I shared a quesadilla with her at a truck stop, and endured her recitation of Juliet's potion scene in her revolting Oklahoma twang. It was simple slipping the arsenic that turned her tequila sunrise into a sunset. I became the respected actress she'd never be. The New York critics rhapsodized over my solo *Three Sisters*. I should have become a major film star but the studios were too busy giving the build up to clap-ridden whores with dubbed voices!

(ominous music begins)

You think you've stopped us, you haven't scratched the surface. We're everywhere, getting stronger, getting three picture deals and producer credit. Listen, hear the drums beating, pounding as we march down Hollywood Boulevard, trampling over the faded names of the soon to be forgotten stars. March! March! Stamp on the infidels, the agents, the bloodsuckers, the columnists! March! March!

R.G. *(to* **YETTA***)* Send her to the psychopathic ward.

*(***YETTA*** begins to lead* **MARTA** *away.)*

MARTA. *(clearly insane)* Who am I? I'm a soviet agent... No, I'm an actress. I'm a soviet agent... No, I'm a seagull. Squawk! Squawk! Masha, want a cracker? *(She lashes out at* **YETTA**.*)* Get away from me, Konstantine Gavrilovitch!

YETTA. *(grabbing hold of her arms)* These nails have to be trimmed.

R.G. Outside Yetta, not on the floor.

(**YETTA** *leads* **MARTA** *off.*)

MARY. And now Frank, what about you?

FRANK. Well, I want to do what's right. But I'm not sure what that is anymore.

MARY. Darling, I think you know what you must do. Come clean.

FRANK. Admit everything?

MARY. Only then can you find true contentment. Pat knows how deadly a secret can be. Don't you, Pat?

PAT. Frank, listen to Pat. Secrets kill.

R.G. Frank, what do you say? You'll speak to the committee?

FRANK. Yeah, sure. I may have just joined the party but hell, I've been pink for years. I'll turn myself in.

MARY. Darling, that's commendable, but don't you think it would be helpful if you gave the names of others we know to be disloyal?

FRANK. Name names? Gee, I don't know if I could.

MARY. My love, leave it to me. I'm in your corner.

FRANK. But what about my childhood friend, the one I killed? It was an accident. I swear it.

MARY. There's no cause for worry. I looked into that too. Your wife has had quite a busy afternoon, and still managed to fit in a photo shoot for *Good Housekeeping*. The bureau knows you were innocent. That's why they never chose to pursue you.

PAT. But what about me, Patricia Maybelle Schmuckleberger? The blood on my hands.

MARY. Pat, you're an American. Remember that. And in our country, only the guilty need live in fear.

(**MARY** *holds both* **FRANK** *and* **PAT** *in her generous embrace, while* **R.G.** *watches with admiration.*)

(*blackout*)

Scene 7

ANNOUNCER. *(voiceover)* The Veedol Motor Oil Program with Pat Pilford.

(applause/music)

(voiceover) Makers of Veedol Motor Oil, found wherever fine cars travel, present Miss Show Business. Pat Pilford. With special guest stars Kate Smith, Dr. Norman Vincent Peale, Music by the West Point Choir and Parker Jones and his Red White and Blue Orchestra, and yours truly, Bill Simmons in what will be my last introduction, since I was fired by Miss Pilford this morning. And now. your fabulous femm-cee, Pat Pilford...

(applause.

PAT. *(in front of her mike down right)* My dear audience. I must depart for a moment from my usual shenanigans, for this is a special day for me and well, for the history of our Union. It's no secret that the lovely film star Mary Dale is my closest and dearest friend. As I speak, she is in Washington, D.C. testifying before the esteemed House Un-American Activities Committee. Some say it's a controversial move on Mary's part. What controversy? The girl's just trying to do her bit. If we don't nip these Bolsheviks in the bud, by golly, by next election day, our White House will be painted red. These people are getting away with murder! Mary, I just want you to know our hearts and prayers are with you. The Lord is thy shepherd. God bless you, Mary Dale.

(MARY enters stage left in a lovely white dress and straw boater. She is the essence of magnificent American womanhood. She is radiant. She crosses to podium.)

(PAT exits stage right door. Behind MARY we see the Capitol Building.)

MARY. *(standing at podium with microphones upstage center)* Senators, gentlemen, only in America could a young girl raised by struggling farmers in Indiana grow up to be a movie star and speak to a distinguished panel of Senators and may I add, most handsome. I hail from a long line of men and women who toiled the land and gave their blood to make this country strong. It is the simple lessons we learn from our forefathers that provide answers to the seemingly complicated questions of today. And so with a clear conscience, I present this committee with a list of names to aid you in your noble hunt to root out the red menace. Together, hands and hearts united, we can make sure these people never work again. *(She opens envelope.)* My, this is exciting. *(She takes list out of envelope.)* I name Marta Towers, Bertram Barker... *(She pauses for a moment, hesitantly.)* and because I love him, Frank Taggart. *(regaining her sense of purpose)* From the student roster of the Yetta Felson Studio, I name Betty Foster, Jeff Patterson, Morris Kleiner, Mildred Pishkin, Lona Myers, Anthony Reaci, Rudy Abbotelli, Howard Mandlebaum, June Sycoff...

(Patriotic music swells and eventually drowns out her speech. Behind the Capitol, a giant flag appears rustling in the breeze. On the stage right side of the flag, a miniature of the Statue of Liberty appears and on stage left of the flag, a miniature of the Liberty Bell. As **MARY** *names names, both the music and lighting become dissonant, disturbing and threatening until both sound and lights suddenly blackout.)*

THE END

COSTUME PLOT

MARY DALE

I-1 Beach house

Green/White Gingham Taffeta Dress w/Green Chiffon

Pleated Overlay & Flower Trim

White Petticoat

White Heels

Corset

Nude Opaque Tights

Rhinestone Necklace

Rhinestone Drop Earrings

Red Wig

I-3 Beach House

Navy Blue Cotton Pajamas w/ "HERS" Embroidery

Mules w/Marabou Puffs

I-4 Bullocks

White Wool Mohair Coat w/Oversized Collar and Buttons

Black Heels

Leopard Wrist Length Gloves

Leopard Pill Box Hat

Gold & Pearl Earrings

Black Patent Clutch

I-5 Felson Studio

White Wool Mohair Coat

Black Heels

Black Velvet Gloves 3/4 Length

Black Velvet Hat w/Multi-colored Porn Porn Trim

Gold Earrings

Black Patent Clutch

II-1 Movie Set

Multi-colored & Mixed Fabric Peasant Dress

Black Heels

Red Wig w/Switch

Flower Wreath w/Ribbon Streamers

II-3 Radio Station

Olive Green Silk Dress w/petticoats

Olive Green/Purple Check Silk Capelet w/Beading

Purple Velvet Hat w/Neil & Pink Flowers

Black Heels

II-4 Beach House/Dream SAME AS II-2 EXCEPT:

    REMOVE: Capelet & Hat

    ADD: Black Patent Clutch

    BEGINNING OF DREAM:

    ADD: Gold Lame Overdress w/Train

    (This goes on over green dress onstage)

    Gold Lame Steeple Hat w/pearl Trim & Scarf

    END OF DREAM:

    Long Red Wig

    White Heels

    No Clothing Except Corset & Tights

II-5 Hospital

    Short Red Wig

    Dressing Robe w/Nightgown Attached

II-6 Felson Studio

    White Wool Mohair Coat

    White Heels

    White Flower Hat w/Neil & Leaf Trim

II-7 Radio Station/ Steps of Congress

    White Dress w/Blue & White Stripe Taffeta Sash

    White Petticoats

    White Straw Hat w/taffeta Trim & Red Flower

    White Heels

    Red French Twist Wig

    Blue Rhinestone Earrings

PAT PILFORD

Prologue Radio Station

    Short Blonde Wig

    Fruit Patterned Dress w/Black Raffia Trim

    Net Polka Dotted Short Overskirt w/Self Bow & Raffia
Trim

    Black Heels

    Black Beaded 3/4 Length Gloves

    Nude Pantyhose

    Black Jet Necklace

    Large White Opalescent Earrings

    Large Black Picture Hat w/Fruit & Raffia Trim

I-1 Beach House

    Same as Prologue

I-3 Bullocks

   Green Dress w/Black Rickrack Trim

   Black Leather Zigzag Belt

   White Opalescent Leather Coat w/Red Rhinestone Pin

   Black Heels

   Large Green Earrings

   Black Jet Necklace

   White Straw Hat w/Black Feathers

   Pink Plastic Purse

   Pink 3/4 Length Gloves

   Large Medallion Bracelet

II-3 Radio Station

   Multi-colored 2 Piece Silk Suit w/Contrasting Fabric Trim & Large
      Bows

   Black Heels

   Blue Rhinestone Earrings

   Blue Rhinestone & Pearl Necklace

   Blue Hat w/Bird & Worm Trim

II-4 Beach House/ Dream

   Court Jester Dress

   Orange Beaded Necklace

   Red Satin Court Jester Hat (No Wig)

   Black Fishnet Tights

   Black Heels

   Black Beaded 3/4 Length Gloves

   Gold Medallion Bracelet

II-5 Hospital (thru the end of the play)

   2 Piece Brown Tweed Suit w/Orange Plaid Taffeta Sash &
   Shoulder Trim

   Short Wrist Length Orange Gloves

   Gold Medallion Bracelet

   Orange Earrings

   Orange Beaded Necklace

   Black Heels

   Large Black Straw Hat

MARTA TOWERS

II-1 Beach House

   Light Blue Dress

   White 3/4 Length Gloves

   Pearl Necklace

White Floral Earrings

2 Petticoats

White Straw Hat

Nude Pantyhose

Blue Plastic Purse

Black/Gray Heels

Page Boy Wig

II-2 The Pier

Royal Blue Patterned Head Scarf

Black Trench Coat

II-5 Felson Studio

Black One-Shouldered Cocktail Dress w/Beading

Opera Length Black Satin Gloves

Black Heels

Black Sequin Earrings

2 Petticoats

II-4 Beach House/Dream

Rust Velvet Gothic Style Dress w/Train

Black Tights

Black Ballet Slippers

Hat w/Chiffon Veil

II-6 Felson Studio

Black/White Tweed Dress

Red Patent Leather Belt

Black Heels

Red Earrings

FRANK TAGGART

I-1 Beach House

Burnt Orange Plaid Sports jacket

White Dress Shirt

Black Pants w/pleats

Black Belt

White V-neck T-shirt

Black Oxfords

Black Socks

I-2 The Pier

Same as 1-1

ADD: Tan Single Breasted Trench Coat

I-3 BEACH HOUSE

Same as 1-1 Except No Sports jacket

I-5 Felson Studio
Green Houndstooth Sports Jacket
Tie
Rest Same As 1-1

II-4 Beach House/ Dream
Pale Gold 50's style Sport Shirt
Black Pants w/Belt
Black Shoes
Black Socks
Red Apron
DURING DREAM:
Blue Velvet Heraldic Overrobe
Prince Valiant Wig
Oversized Velvet Hat w/Jewel Trim

II-5 Hospital
White Shirt
Tie
Burnt Orange Plaid Sports Jacket
Black Pants
Belt
Black Shoes
Black Socks

II-6 Felson Studio
Repeat II-5

RALPH BARNES

Prologue Radio Station
White T-shirt
Red/White Plaid Shirt
BluelYellow/White Searsucker Plaid Vest
Red Paisley Bowtie
Black Socks
Brown Wing Tip Oxfords
Brown Tweed Suit Pants w/Belt
Gray Fedora
Moustache

Sales Girl

I-4 Bullocks
Nude Opaque Tights
Black Dress w/White Collar & Cuffs
Black Belt

Black Petticoat
Black Heels
Brunette Wig
Black Glasses w/Pearl Chain Guard
Pearl/Gold Earrings
Pearl Bracelet
Gardenia Corsage

R. G. BENSON

I-5 Felson Studio
White Turtleneck
Brown Tweed Suit Pants w/Belt
Brown Tweed Suit Jacket
Brown Wingtip Oxfords
Black Socks

II-2 Movie Set
White Shirt
Orange/Brown Patterned Ascot
Brown Herringbone Tweed Norfolk Jacket
Brown Tweed Suit Pants w/Belt
Brown Wingtip Oxfords
Black Socks

II-6 Felson Studio
Brown Tweed Suit
White Shirt
Brown/Orange Stripe Tie
Black Socks
Brown Wingtip Shoes

GRANNY LOU

II-4 Beach House/ Dream
Blue/Red Patterned House Dress
Nude Tights
Knitted Shawl
Red Wig
Black "Old Lady" Shoes

JERRY

Prologue Radio Station
Blue Overalls
White T-shirt
Black Socks
Black Wingtip Oxfords
Moustache

BERTRAM BARKER

I-5 Felson Studio

Gray Glen Plaid 2-Piece Single-Breasted Suit

White Button Down Shirt

T-shirt

Black Socks

Black Wingtip Shoes

Blue & Red Patterned Tie

II-4 Beach House/ Dream

Brown Heraldic Underrobe

Orange Velvet Overrobe w/Fur Trim

Brown Sandals

II-6 Felson Studio

Same Suit & Shirt

Blue/Rose Patterned Tie

T-shirt

Black Socks

Black Wingtip Shoes

MITCHELL DRAKE

I-4 Bullocks

Gray 2-Piece Single-Breasted Suit

Beige Shirt

Yellowl/Rust Patterned Tie

Black Socks

T-shirt

Black Shoes

Tan Trenchcoat

Gray Fedora

I-5 Felson Studio

Same as 1-4 But Loose

II-2 Telephone Booth

Gray 2-Piece Single-Breasted Suit

Pink Shirt

Dusty Pink & Red Patterned Tie

Black Socks

T-shirt

Black Shoes

Tan Trenchcoat

Gray Fedora

II-4 *Beach House/ Dream*
Gray Felt & Chainmail Tunic
Chainmail Leggings & Feet
Helmet
Sword
II-6 *Felson Studio*
Gray 2-Piece Single-Breasted Suit
Pink Shirt
Red Tie
Black Shoes
Black Socks
T-Shirt
Gray Fedora

MALCOLM

I-1 *Beach House*
White Shirt
Black Bow Tie
Black Tux Pants
Black Socks
Black Penny Loafers
White "Major Domo" Jacket
I-3 *Beach House*
Red/Black Plaid Robe
Brown Slippers
I-5 *Felson Studio*
Navy Blue Long-Sleeved Sport Shirt w/Elastic Waistband
Bronze Pants w/Cuff
Black Socks
Black Penny Loafers
II-2 *Telephone Booth*
Same as 1-5 With Addition of Navy Blue Golf Jacket
II-4 *Beach House/ Dream*
Black Tights
Monks Robe
Monks Hooded Tabbard
Rope Belt
Wooden Bead Necklace w/Cross
Brown Slippers
II-2 *Hospital*
Repeat II-2

RUDY

II-I Movie Set

Cream Short-sleeved Sport Shirt
Medium Blue Pants w/Cuffs
Blonde Wig
Black Socks
Black Loafers
Black Glasses

OLD LADY

II-6 Felson Studio

Monks Robe
Black Tights
Maroon Embroidered Overrobe
White Wig
Black Dance Shoes
Various Necklaces

PROPERTY PLOT

NOTE: The screen "panel" on tracking plays in various positions throughout the entire show.

PROLOGUE-RADIO STATION
"On the Air" sign (Fly in)

Stand microphone

Door slam unit

Script pages (pat, Ralph, Jerry)

Cigarette (Jerry)

I-1 BEACH HOUSE (TEA PARTY)
Chair unit

Valance unit (Fly in)

Settee/coffee table unit w/cigarette container, lighter & ashtray

Platter w/lamp, phone, ash tray

Platter w/liquor tray including:

Ice bucket w/cubes & tongs

Martini shaker

Scotch bottle

Cigarette lighter, cigarettes

1 Tumbler

1 Ash tray

Passport (Mary)

Pack of cigarettes, pocket Zippo lighter (Frank)

Tea tray (Malcolm) with:

   3 Cups & saucers

   1 Spoon

   Teapot

   Cream pitcher (empty)

   Sugar bowl w/cubes & tongs; no top

   Plate w/3 crumpets & 3 tea cookies

   3 Cloth napkins under plate

I-2 THE PIER
Pack of cigarettes & pocket Zippo Lighter (Frank)

Smoke machine

I-3 THE BEACH HOUSE (LATE NIGHT)
Repeat platters, chair, settee/table

Set of house keys (Frank)

Passport (Mary)

Pillow & blanket (Mary)

I-4 BULLOCKS

Compact (in Pat's purse)

Sales book w/pencil (Sales Girl)

Eye glasses on chain (Sales Girl)

Porn Porn hat (Sales girl)

Stock of "shopping" boxes (Mary)

2 Garments on hangers (Mary)

Set pieces:

Fabric swag (Ay in)

Side fabric panels (swing out from SR & SL door units)

1-5 FELSON STUDIO OFFICE

Furniture/set pieces:

Desk unit w/blotter & ash tray attached

File cabinet unit

Rolling office chair

Hanging office lamp

Curtain SR doorway

Letter opener (trick knife) velcroed to desk top

Acting contract (in desk slot)

Karl Marx book (in desk pouch)

Oblong tray w/6 shot glasses & vodka bottle

Cigar (Barker)

Writing pen. dry (Barker)

Pipe. tobacco. lighter (R.G.)

Pack of cigarettes. lighter (Mitchell)

Party membership card (Malcolm): gets tom up each performance

II-1 MOVIE SOUND STAGE

Movie kleig light on stand

Director chair

Fire bucket

Ladder

Movie clapper

Cigarette (Mary)

Vial of pills (R.G.)

Boom Mic "Shadow"

II-2 PHONE BOOTH

Period pay phone

5¢ slugs (Malcolm)

Crumpled piece of paper (Malcolm)

Pack of cigarettes & Zippo pocket lighter (Mitchell)

II-3 RADIO STATJON
Standing mic
Script pages (Mitchell gives to Pat)
Script pages (Mary)
Handkerchief (Mitchell)

II-4 BEACH HOUSE THROUGH DREAM
Basic furniture units (repeat)
On coffee table:
  Ash tray
  Cigarette lighter
  Cigarette container
  "Cousin Bette" book
  Box w/necklace
  Platter w/phone, ash tray & lamp
  Platter w/liquor tray, scotch bottle
Apron (Frank)
2nd vial of pills (in Mary's purse)
2 Banners (pages)
Kitchen towel (Granny Lou)
The horse (from trap in platform)
Vac and smoke machine

II-5 HOSPITAL
Bed
Bible
Folding screen

II-6 FELSON STUDIO OFFICE
Furniture: repeat except arm chair
Letter opener (trick knife) velcroed to desk
File folders (in desk slot)
School roster list (in desk slot)
"Project Pilford" file folder with pictures (in file cabinet)
Sealed letter (Mitchell)
Cigar (Barker)
Post card & FBI badge (R.G.)

II-7 RADIO into CAPITAL
Bank of microphones (1 real)
Envelope w/list (Mary)
Set Pieces:
Flag, Capitol cut out, Liberty Bell & Statue of Liberty (cut outs on
  track)

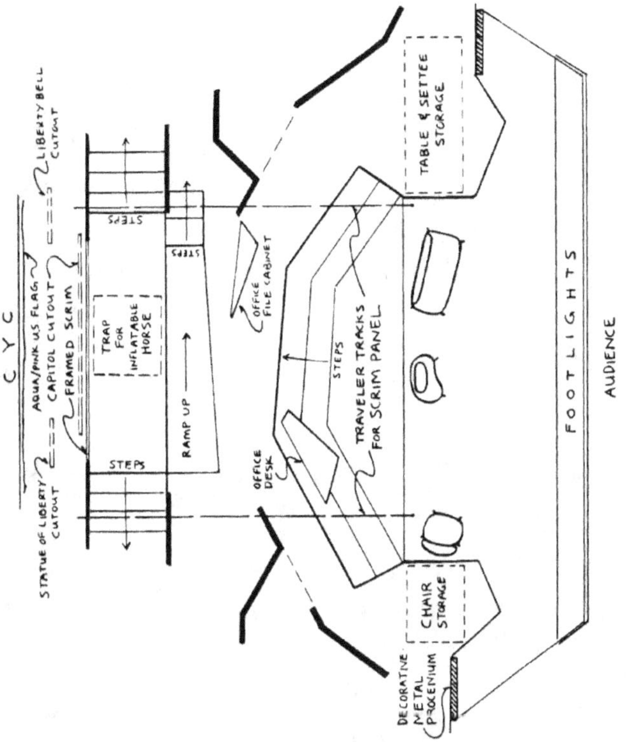

GROUND PLAN

DESIGNER: BTWhitehill...

OFFICE

BEACH HOUSE

L.LORTEL THEATRE, NY, NY SET DESIGN: B Whitehill...   PHOTOS: TL BOSTON